muse

new york times bestselling author

katy evans

This book is a work of fiction. Any reference to historical events, real people, or real places are used fictitiously. Other names, characters, places, and events are products of the author's imagination, and any resemblance to actual events or places or persons, living or dead, is entirely coincidental.

First paperback edition: August 2018

Cover design by Sara Hansen at Okay Creations
Interior formatting by JT Formatting

10 9 8 7 6 5 4 2 1

Library of Congress Cataloguing-in-Publication Data is available

ISBN-13: 978-1724590541
ISBN-13: (ebook) 978-1732443914

To the muse

table of contents

playlist

"On the Loose" – Niall Horan
"Accidentally in Love" – Counting Crows
"Superheroes" – The Script
"Something Just Like This" – Chainsmokers and Coldplay
"Strangers in Love" – Parisian
"Ride" – Lana del Rey
"Open" – Rhye
"One Call Away" – Charlie Puth
"All I Want" – Kodaline
"Too Much to Ask" – Niall Horan

chapter one

Becka

New York can be a cruel, cruel city.

To me, anyway.

I came here to cheer up my best friend, Bryn, who was going through a bad breakup.

But now she's back with her man. Mission accomplished. Yes!

I also wanted to research and finish my romance novel.

I just didn't.

Why? Because I suck. I didn't really do much of anything. Except if you count wondering why my muse wouldn't cooperate.

I did that *a lot.*

Now I'm heading back home, hoping that my bitch muse will come back and get playing.

Keep talking to me like that and I'm leaving for good, I can almost hear Bitch Muse say.

Sighing as I get my last good glimpse of the city I barely tasted, I spot my Uber pulling over and haul my suitcase to the curb.

The driver steps out to grab my luggage and puts it inside the trunk.

I climb in the back, and we're on our way to JFK. I drink in as much as I can of the busy streets that chewed me up and spit me out as we head out of the city. Manhattan. The Big Apple. New Fucking York.

I'd really wanted to explore. See the sights. Get some inspiration. I'm in the middle of my book—aka Best Love Story Ever—and I got stuck when the characters fought. It's the big black moment, and I made it happen. I know, I'm so proud. I'm God in my own little world, which I *love.*

But now I have no idea how to fix it, to draw them out of the big black pit of despair. Ben, my hero, is acting like an asshole. Leia, my heroine, is a pain in my ass. I was sure that going out and absorbing a city like New York would cure me of anything, especially writer's block.

But Bryn was too busy with the launch of her House of Sass enterprise. Her roommate Sara has been banging some rich mogul dude and hardly came home. I was certain that a big girl like me, independent and with her pants strapped on correctly, would have no trouble going out on her own exploring Manhattan.

Well, I did. I rented myself a hotel room for two weeks and went out and explored.

And got lost when I went to Chelsea, to the Meatpacking District.

I got yelled at by cab drivers, passersby, and even some stupid barista at a café when I couldn't decide what I wanted to eat in a second flat.

Turns out, things move really fast in this city. I felt humiliated, confused, and in the end, wondered if I was the same girl that thought she had her pants on straight when she left Austin.

This city? It doesn't seem to think I've got on anything straight, from my pants to my brain.

Truth is, I'm not sure I like New York. It just wasn't what I expected, it didn't give me what I needed…and I'm pretty sure New York doesn't like me back.

Checking my phone for messages (I've got nil), I suppose it'll be a good thing to go back home. Maybe being away from the grind will make me appreciate it more.

I miss my cat Tibby, and I also miss the quiet. It's noisy here, so noisy it's hard to hear yourself think. It's also colder than I like it, definitely colder than in Austin. I miss my usual Starbucks café where the barista greets me with a smile and always knows what I want and has it ready by the time I walk in and head to my writing corner. Except my writing corner has been uninspiring lately—and my well, yes, my BITCH muse hasn't shown up since I somehow fabricated this whole dramatic black moment between stupid Ben and stupid Leia. Ugh.

On my way home, I text my sister Lily.

Lily: ***How's the book? All wrapped up?***

Me: ***HA! More like about to be dumped into the smelliest, closest New York dumpster.***

Lily: ***Haha. You can do it. You were so excited about this trip***

Me: ***Was is the keyword. The city is crazy and I seem to be more incompetent than I'd like to let myself believe. Could hardly go out on my own without getting trampled or nearly run over. It's a jungle I tell you***

Lily: ***Aww. Well you'll be home soon. The place you so anxiously wanted to ESCAPE! The one you called your jail!***

Me: ***Whatever. I was being dramatic. That's what writers do when they can't figure out their books. They create drama in their own lives from out of nothing. What about you?***

Lily: ***Taking the bar tomorrow. Bleh. Oh! Saw Trevor on Dirty 6th this weekend***

Ugh. I did not want to hear the T-word.

I think of asking Lily what he looked like. Who he was with. Whether he asked about me.

But I already know the answers. A) hot, B) a bunch of his college frat brothers, C) no.

Sigh. He was the boy who made me want to spew poetry and made writing the first half of my novel a breeze. We dated for three weeks, and I'd never been so inspired.

Then he cheated on me. Stupid Trevor.

It's been four months. I should've gotten my mojo back by now. Or at least gotten back into the dating scene. Nope.

So, I just finish with: ***Good luck, not that you'll need it. You'll slay it***

My little sister doesn't need the luck. She's brilliant, top of her class at UT Law. She's the one who all my family used to look at and say, "That girl. She's gonna make something of herself!"

And then there's me. The *other* one.

I head to the gate and take a seat, pulling my laptop from my carry-on and rereading the last paragraph I'd written. Chapter nineteen, which I've been stuck on for…oh, four months.

Then I delete, delete, delete.

Stupid. Pathetic. A bunch of monkeys left in a room with my laptop probably could've done better.

I have a feeling people are laughing at me. I glance around, then peer at the screen near the gate. St. Louis, departing at eight p.m.

What? What happened to Dallas Fort Worth, the first leg of my connecting flight to Austin?

I set my laptop on the chair beside me and head to the counter. "Ma'am…"

"One moment." She halts me, typing in something at her keyboard.

I breathe and count to ten.

She looks up. "Yes?"

"The screen's wrong. Isn't this the flight to Dallas?"

"Flight to Dallas?" She looks at me as if I've sprouted horns. "Oh no. The gate was changed."

Shit. "Changed where?"

She types some stuff and gives me the new gate.

"And where's that?" I ask, near hyperventilating.

"It's boarding now, so you're going to have to do a whole lot of running. You have to get to Concourse C. This is Concourse B."

I'm only half-listening as she spits out directions. I don't know how I do it, but within two seconds I've run back to my place, grabbed all my stuff and run a sprint that would've won me a medal somewhere.

I slide into the gate like a baserunner and see my plane still outside. I exhale in relief, but then I notice the doors are shut.

Like a dumbass, I try to pry open the door, even though there isn't a handle.

"Miss…you can't go in there. You're too late."

"No, I'm—"

The woman at the podium points outside. The plane is already easing back.

"Oh no, no!" I groan. "Nobody told me the gate changed!"

The lady behind the podium looks at me like, *Did you read the screen, dummy?* "We changed it an hour ago. We made an announcement."

I stomp around and circle angrily, shaking my head because I'm going to have to wait here for who knows how many hours, plus am I going to have to pay for another ticket? I'm not that rich right now considering I've got a useless Best Love Story Ever sitting in my laptop. I pace back and forth, thinking of my empty checking account.

"Please tell them to stooooop," I beg.

"We can't. I'm sorry."

I'm turning around, glancing down at my carry-on items as a voice yells, "Hold the plane!"

A guy is charging toward the doors. I don't realize I'm in the guy's way until we're stumbling in the aisle together, like a Twister game gone wrong.

"Sorry," he apologizes, his hand snaking out to grab me. I shiver and don't know if it's a good thing or a bad, and my skin feels weirdly branded where he touched me as he steps toward the podium.

"Hey! Hold the plane?" he grits it out as a question, like, *Didn't you hear me the first time?*

"Sorry—" She points at the moving aircraft as it taxies out of the gate.

"Fuck. It." The guy steps back, as agitated as I was a second ago, and plunges a hand into his rumpled, sandy hair. He shakes his head side to side, his jaw working mercilessly. "Fuck. Me."

Fuck. Everything? My sentiments exactly.

He drops his bag and kicks it, then throws a beaten leather jacket down atop it. Dragging a hand down his jaw, he beelines to the window and watches. He fists his hair in one hand, his knuckles white, shaking his head again as he comes back, grabs his carry-on and jacket, and drops them on one of the empty chairs.

He collapses in the chair next to it, crosses his arms, and sighs.

I feel a little sorry for him. I'm tempted to go and tell him I know just how he feels, but he seems more pissed off than normal, and I decide I'm irritated on my own without having to deal with someone else's anger.

I take a page from his book though. I sit, my back to him, as I text my sister. ***I missed my flight!***

The guy makes a phone call.

"Hey… I know you won't like this but…tomorrow morning's not looking good. Yeah. I missed my flight out of JFK."

He sounds deeply peeved. I wonder who he's talking to. If it's a girlfriend, he sounds like he hates her.

Trying not to eavesdrop, I peer into my bag, and—didn't I put my laptop there? I panic as I shuffle all my belongings inside.

It's not there.

My laptop

Is

Not

There.

I spring to my feet and head to where I was standing only moments ago, retracing my steps in growing apprehension. It's not anywhere. Where the fuck is my laptop?

I start hyperventilating—and this isn't good. I have anxiety—which has been known to be crippling from time to time. I suppose it's because I rarely go out of the house. Writer, solitary business, yada yada yada. So when I do go out, and anything does not go to plan, my lungs begin failing, my heart palpitating, my palms sweating.

Like…now.

I feel the familiar choking sensation of my windpipe closing, and my eyes begin to sting in frustration. *God. No, not here, not now, please!*

The guy hangs up and spots me. Everyone spots me, because I'm breathing like an animal in labor, about five seconds away from falling to the ground into fetal position, like a poked pill bug.

His lips move in slow motion. I can't hear anything because my heartbeat is a drum in my ears. But I think it's, "What's up your butt?"

"I..." I fight for words. "I lost my laptop. Did you see it?"

I glance at his bags, desperate for any sign of my laptop.

My laptop is my life.

My work, my stories, *my life.*

I close my eyes, and it helps. I calm down. My heartbeat slows.

"I didn't steal your laptop."

I open my eyes and scowl at him.

"I'm not accusing you!" I cry, exasperated. "I'm just asking—" I clutch my stomach. Oh god, I may have written the story in weeks, when I was with Trevor, but I spent four months tweaking it—and now it's all gone. I've never been good about backing my stuff up. And in that laptop are all the starts of other books, *my whole life.* Poof. Gone.

Dormant Bitch Muse has left the building.

He has his arms crossed, and is stroking his chin, like he's trying to understand me, but I'm speaking gibberish. "Well, what are you trying to say?"

"You don't understand." I tap on the podium frantically until the busy attendant looks up. "Please, can you ask if I left a laptop over at Gate 2? It'll take me ages to get there and I want to be sure no one steals it by the time I—"

"You think whoever found it will return it to you?"

I pause at the sardonic laughter in the voice behind me. I whirl around and glare. "I...yes."

"Whoa. You're not from around here, are you?"

I scan him from head to toe. Despite being intent on crushing my hopes, the guy is pretty darn gorgeous. A little disheveled looking. His hair standing this way and that. His gray t-shirt hugging muscles that would make any woman's knees weak.

But gorgeous does not equal all-knowing. There are plenty of good Samaritans in the world. And I shall prove it, right now.

"No. I'm not from here. Thus the airport," I snap, pulling my eyes away from his gorgeous muscles. I focus on the attendant. "*Please.*"

She holds up a finger and picks up a phone. She converses briefly with someone on the other end, then hangs up. "I'm sorry. No laptop at Gate 2."

It takes all my restraint to keep from lunging over the podium and grabbing her lapels. "Please. Can you make an announcement or something? I'll offer a reward. I need that laptop back!"

Suddenly, the palpitations become a squeezing in my chest. I gasp as my breath becomes shallow and fast. My windpipe constricts on me. My vision bends.

Oh, no.

The floor under my feet waves, bringing me to my knees, and my hands scrabble around, grasping at a whole lot of nothing. Nausea rolls over me, and when I raise my head lights blink back at me, blurrier as the darkness starts coming.

That's it. I'm dying. I'm dying, and now Leia and Ben will never have their happy ending. I guess it serves them right for being assholes, but still. I gasp "help" when I feel a woman's hand on my shoulders and smell her rosy perfume.

"Are you all right? This girl needs help!"

"She's with me," a familiar voice says. Someone hands me a paper bag, and the voice says, "Breathe."

I start breathing into the bag, and my throat begins to open up again. My pulse rate slows.

I try to stand, my mind ragged as I hold onto the first thing I can grab. It's a solid, hard arm and once I'm assured that I'm standing on my own, I let go but sway. The hand comes back. I gasp again because even in my state, the touch causes my body to immediately contract.

I glance up at the guy—that same guy who missed his flight, whose lips are now curling in a devilish grin.

"You all right?"

How can some stranger make it all better, make me feel as if I'm safe?

I try to step back, but he tightens his hold as I nod nervously.

"You sure?"

I continue nodding faster, his eyes trekking my face in assessment as he drags his hand over my back, as if making sure I'm okay. I'm definitely okay, but affected, affected by this guy in ways that confound me.

"You can let go now."

He raises one eyebrow at me. "Your body doesn't want me to." He glances pointedly at my fingers, digging into his bicep.

"I…ah…" I try to pry them free, and when I hear a slow chuckle, I jerk my face back.

"What's so funny?"

I tilt my chin up as the guy studies me. He's ridiculously close, and I can smell him. He smells yummy and exciting, comforting and like danger all at once.

"You can't help it, can you?" he asks, running a hand down my arm, watching as my flesh pebbles.

I snatch back my arm. "You're a dick."

"A dick who just saved you from kissing airport tile." When I just gape at him, he says, "You're welcome."

Total dick, with a cherry on top.

I blink and look around. Still no laptop.

I was hoping that was just a bad nightmare.

The guy's still looking at me, a grin of amusement on his face. Dick with cherry *and* whipped cream.

Oh god, I don't need the mental image that's creating in my head. Like the guy isn't lickable enough without it. "And by the way, I'm not *with* you."

He shrugs. "Okay, fine."

I make a move toward the podium, and he does at the exact same time. We end up tangling together again, my shoulder bumping against his broad chest. He holds his hands up, palms out, and lets me go first.

How the fuck is it that in one of the world's biggest airports, we keep butting heads?

I mean, he has a very nice head, but still…

Podium lady is getting pretty miffed at me by now. I can tell by the look on her face. "I know, I know. No laptop. But… when's the next flight to Austin?"

She types in some stuff and shakes her head. "Direct? Not until tomorrow evening."

Tomorrow evening? FML. "But—"

"And it's a full flight, so you'd be on standby. Storms down south cancelled a lot of flights. You could take a connecting flight with a layover in Raleigh Durham or Dallas tomorrow morning. They'll get you to Austin a little earlier."

I groan and hand her my ID. "Fine. Just…put me on the connecting flight through Dallas."

"There's a two-hundred dollar fee for that."

Of course there is. I hand her my suffering, overused credit card.

I get my new ticket and step aside. I check my phone for the time.

Only…sixteen hours to kill. Fantastic.

At first, I think this could be good. Maybe I can just sit somewhere quiet and force myself to write.

But then it hits me.

My laptop is still missing.

Damn damn damn. I open a text to Lily who still hasn't responded to my last rant: ***And my laptop is gone. I may die here at JFK.***

I watch hot annoying guy leaning over the podium, as he talks to the woman. He strikes me as familiar, but I can't think of from where.

When he finishes, two cool, ashy-gray eyes focus on me.

I look back at my phone, ignoring him.

"Hey," he says. "We're on the same flight. Let's not fuck this one up, shall we?"

I harrumph at him. "I plan not to."

"Want to get out and see the city?"

I frown at him. "That's presumptuous of you to think I'd go anywhere with you just because…"

"Because you react to my touch in a way that excites the bloody daylights out of me?" he asks, not smiling, his gaze intent. "I actually think we should go straight to bed and explore that a little more, don't you?"

I struggle to gain my composure. But this guy exudes cockiness, a devil's attitude, and a shit ton of confidence.

"I'm not going anywhere with you."

He laughs at me like *that's* the more absurd option than sharing a bed with him, a stranger. "You're staying here all night? Doing what?"

I have plenty to do. One, find my laptop. Two, FIND MY LAPTOP. Three, make damned sure I'm the first one at the gate tomorrow. The right gate. I can't afford to have another panic attack.

But the last thing I need to do is explain myself to Cocky McCockerson. "Things."

He looks at me with that lopsided smile that simultaneously makes my heart skip and annoys me. "Mysterious. I like that. Like what?"

"All I know is they don't include sleeping with you."

I exhale, trembling, still, after my panic attack—or maybe the way this guy unsettles me.

"So…which is it? Do you really love JFK, or do you really hate Manhattan?"

"Neither, I just—"

"Because sleeping on these chairs doesn't sound fun. A hotel room—"

"I don't need a room. I have friends in New York," I huff, looking around for a comfortable, out of the way place to collapse and spend the next sixteen hours.

"Good for you. But one thing your friends don't have? Me."

Wait. Before, I'd thought he was just joking, being a cocky asshole. Is he seriously insinuating that I'd get a room with him? Really?

His eyes twinkle, and yep. That's exactly what he's saying.

It probably works for him, too. I notice he keeps getting glances from all the women around him. He slides on a baseball cap, and I can only see his lips. What pretty pink lips, for a man.

God I want that mouth on me.

What are you thinking, Becka? Did the panic attack get into your head?

"Let's get one thing straight," I say to him. "You can go wherever you like. But I'm staying here. I'm not leaving without my laptop. And I'm definitely not sharing a room—or a bed, or *anything*—with you."

A bold gaze traps me. "What's got you so peeved?"

"My laptop. I'm a writer. My whole life is inside there."

"It can't be. If it were, you wouldn't be sitting here, all gorgeous and riled up next to me. You look perfectly fine to me."

I shoot him a dark look. "Do those lines actually work for you?"

"Come now. Or when we get to the hotel." He grins. "You can relax, whatever you lost can be regained."

"No, it can't. It's all on my hard drive."

"Then you'll replace it with something better."

His hard cock, I'm sure. He certainly thinks a lot about himself.

With good reason.

I clench my teeth. I hate myself for having those thoughts about him because he can clearly read my mind, just as easy as he can read the way I'm blushing from head to toe, or the way his touch flips my switch to ON.

"Like, hello? NEVER."

He shrugs, confident, and says, "You want it as much as I do," as he stretches his hands over his head, baring a sliver of cut, tan stomach.

Holy lord.

This buffet of eye candy simply can't be real.

In my books, Leia always has a comeback ready. But it takes me a moment to recover. More than a moment. I practically have to pick my tongue up off the floor.

"You delude yourself. You're probably so used to women throwing themselves at you that you've never seen one who doesn't."

"And yet I remember pulling you up to your feet just now…and never having watched anyone respond to me like you just did."

I suck in a breath and glower at him. "I admit, you made me lose my head, but that doesn't mean I can't recover. See? All better. Now go on to your hotel room and leave me alone."

"Aw, Rebecca. After we shared such a nice time together."

I stare at him. "How did you…"

"I may have seen your ID when you booked your ticket."

"Oh, okay. Creep. Is that how you pick up women?"

"Pretty much."

To be honest, nobody uses Rebecca. It sounds so serious and important, so mature. But I don't want him to call me Becka. I want him to think I'm mature, to respect me. He's using every line in the book to try to coax me into bed. So… why do I want him to respect me, again?

Because he's hot as hell and does things to my body that make me not respect myself?

"Thank you for helping me out back there. That was… surprising…"

"You'll find I'm full of surprises, Rebecca." He nods, smiling while he eyes me intimately. "So many I hope you don't discover them all."

He reaches out, touches my lips, and I gasp and physically react to him again.

Good heavens, this man is going to kill me.

chapter two

Noah

The lady doth protest too much, methinks.

It's been a day.

A shitty day.

I'd wanted to take a bite out of the Big Apple, making my mark on Broadway and showing off my acting chops.

Instead, I feel like the Big Apple took a bite out of my ass.

You're a little too pretty and buff to be our Hamlet.

What the actual fuck? Too pretty? Wasn't that what make-up was for? And buff? I was not buff in any sense of the word. She had to be thinking of my CGI-enhanced body. Besides, wouldn't their Hamlet be clothed?

Disastrous audition aside, I had my agent, Anne, book me the first flight home so that I could make it back to L.A. in time to get make-up for my latest release's publicity shots.

"I know it's a pain in the ass," I say as I wait in line at Starbucks. "But we'll just have to reschedule."

Can't say I'm unhappy about not having to spend four hours in the chair tomorrow, getting blue. But I'm going to have to get them over with eventually.

It's in my contract.

As is three more years of this bullshit, it seems.

Not that I don't appreciate Megalith. Megalith is my bread and butter. The reason I can post rent each month and then some.

The big blue guy might be a superhero, but he's also a bit of an asshole, since he's taken over my life.

Anne sighs audibly. "I just checked Expedia. There's a direct flight leaving from JFK tonight. JetBlue. What about that one?"

"No. You know I don't do Blue."

"Make. An. Exception." She sounds truly exasperated to me. But I'm her gravy train, so she has to put up with me. "Oh. Here's one with Delta."

"Anne. No. I'm booked on the eleven-twenty-five tomorrow afternoon with American. I'll be in before midnight."

"Why would you want to take a connection? There are non-stop flights—"

"Anne." My eyes trail over to Rebecca, who's talking to a janitor. Explaining her lost laptop woes, obviously, from the way she's gesturing like the sky is about to cave in.

"All right. All right. Was the audition that bad?"

I frown. "Yeah."

Ten years ago, after a performance as a drug-addicted teen baseball player in a little-known indie flick, *Going Home,* that got Oscar short-listed, I was the talk of Hollywood. I followed it up with two more roles that got me a lot of praise. No money, but a lot of praise. *People* magazine named me number three on their Ones to Watch list.

And then my agent plopped the Galaxy Titans franchise on my desk.

A six-movie series.

They wanted me to star as the alter ego of meek and chubby Andrew Steuben, a superhero named Megalith, who has abs to die for and can crush mountains just by thinking of it.

For a million dollars a movie.

Hell, yes.

It would require a lot of make-up, and I'd be enhanced by CGI, of course. But I didn't care. I needed the money. I signed on the dotted line.

The Galaxy Titans franchise is now one of the biggest movie franchises ever.

Noah Steele is almost a household name. But I'm never recognized on the street. Never asked to sign autographs unless I'm at an official press appearance.

Which kind of fucking takes the fun out of being a movie star.

You know how often these days I get recognized from my earlier work, the work I'm most proud of? Never.

Also: No one ever told me that when I signed up to play a superhero, those juicy parts? The ones that could make people take me as a serious actor? A leading man? Gone.

Now, all I've got to do is show up, get blue, and flash my six-pack.

So that's all I am. A hot, blue piece of eye-candy. And most of that is with the help of CGI.

So really, I'm nothing.

Two years ago, when I saw the six-movie series coming to an end, I asked my agent to look into more serious roles and get me back to my roots. She sent out word that I was open for new roles.

I didn't get a bite. Not a single audition.

Not one.

Anne suggested that I should take a rest from Hollywood. After two years of looking, word out on the street was that I was desperate. She suggested I check out Broadway, since I'd gotten my start in high school and college working theater.

Then she told me that the Galaxy Titans franchise wanted to sign me on for another three movies.

I hate to bite the hand that feeds me. But…after *King of the Galaxy*, releasing this December…I'm done.

I can't be typecast as that blue asshole.

Can't. Won't.

"Aw," Anne says to me. "It's just one audition. There will be more. I hear a new production of *Rent* is looking for a Roger."

I scrub my hand over my face as I get to the front of the line. I mouth my order for two Venti coffees. "When?"

"Auditions start next week."

I played Roger in college. I know that role like the back of my hand. It's a meaty, emotional role. "I guess. Yeah. Sure. Sign me up."

"I will. But Noah?" A silence. "Get back here fast. I know you hate these films and that I had to twist your arm to get you to start promoting them some more. But please."

"Right." I end the call, pocket the phone, and walk over to where Rebecca is slumped in a chair. "No one has seen my laptop," she moans.

I set the coffee in the cup holder next to her. “Here.”

She looks up at me. I’ve never met a woman who was equal parts sexy and cute like she is. She’s tiny and pixie-like, her hair up in this messy bun that looks like she just slept on it. Everything about her says, *Come to bed.* The only big things on her are her emerald eyes—bedroom eyes, if ever I saw them—and two pouty pink lips.

Lips I’ve wanted to taste since the moment she fainted into my arms.

After that, getting on Broadway stopped being a priority. Getting that taste? That’s my goal.

She lifts the cover on her coffee and stares into it like it holds the secrets of the universe. “Weren’t you going to a hotel?”

I sit next to her. “I would’ve. If you came with me. Now there’s no point. I’ve already fucked myself enough today. I was looking for someone else.”

“Not. Happening.”

I sip my coffee. “It could, though.”

“Seriously. No.”

Like I said, she’s protesting way too much. I’m onto her. Especially after the way she turned on for me. Every pore prickling with goosebumps, nipples pressing through her thin t-shirt, that look in those green eyes that said, *Take me.*

She stands up and grabs her bag. “I’m going to the TSA office. That’s where the lost and found is. Thanks for the coffee, but I’ve got to…”

I stand up, following her as she kicks up the pace and starts to hurry toward the front of the terminal. For a little thing, she moves fast.

She stops when I catch up to her. "Did I forget something else?"

"No. I thought I could help you. Find your laptop."

"How?"

"You know. Four eyes are better than two."

She rolls her eyes. "I guess."

She keeps walking and I follow beside her. "So, you're a writer? What kind of stuff do you write?"

"Romance. I came to New York to research my book and finish it."

"Did you?"

"No."

"Why not?"

She exhales. "Writer's block, I guess."

"So you're telling me you came to research a romance. I offer you a night of unbridled passion. And you turned me down…why, again?"

Her mouth quirks up in a smile. "I mean, that's such an appetizing offer. But Ben and Leia would never just hop into bed like that."

"Ben and Leia?"

"My main characters. That would be the first chapter. Theirs is a slow-burn love. They didn't even kiss until chapter twelve."

"Are you kidding me? Sounds dull. With the chemistry you and I have, I bet we won't hold out until chapter three."

She wrinkles her nose in disgust, but the way her pupils dilate and her breath comes faster betrays her. "You are not my Ben."

"And why's that?"

"Because he has dark hair. And he wears a suit. He's a billionaire, an artist, and a humanitarian. But as successful and talented as he is, he doesn't have an ego at all. He's a gentleman."

"So he's a stiff?" She whirls to face me, a frown on her face as if I insulted her real boyfriend. Before she can protest, I add, "So, are you Leia?"

Her frown softens and becomes a smile. She's gorgeous in an imperfect way, her hair frizzing out of her band like a halo, a tiny space between her front teeth. Not L.A. plastic or New York pretention. She's natural.

I have the overwhelming urge to rip that band out of her hair and pull her to me.

"I guess. She's the person I want to be. Kind. Friendly. Loved by everyone who knows her. But really beautiful and sexy. Ben can't resist her."

"I'm not sure I can speak for the other ones, but you *are* really sexy. I'm having a hard time resisting you."

She gives me a doubtful look. "No. That is one place where Leia and I are definitely different."

"So you think. But I'm serious."

"I don't really need one-liners. What I need is for my bitch muse to fall in line and start giving me the goods."

"Bitch muse?"

She nods as we get to the door that says TSA. It's empty in there, except for a woman in a blue sweater behind the desk who is playing with her cell phone and looks like she doesn't want to be disturbed.

"Excuse me," Rebecca says to the lady. "Has anyone turned in a Mac Air in a hot pink case? It would've come in within the hour."

The woman frowns without looking up and pushes a pad of paper over to her. "Sorry. Fill this form out and if it comes in, we'll notify you."

"Thanks." Sighing, she hunches over the desk and starts to write. I lean next to her, watching. When she finishes and slides the form over, she sighs. "Bitch muse. The voice inside me who has been strangely silent for the past...oh, four months?"

"*Four* months?" I repeat. "Shit. That's serious."

She gives me a look that says, *You're telling me.*

"Where to now?" I ask.

She scans the busy terminal, filled with frantic people with places to go. On the contrary, the two of us have fifteen hours to kill. We wind up wandering to the nearest duty-free shop, selling perfume and liquor and a lot of other shit I have no interest in.

She reaches over and sniffs a cologne, then wrinkles her cute pixie nose. I take it and sniff. Her assessment was correct. It's putrid. "For your boyfriend?" I inquire.

She ignores me and sniffs another one.

I lift a glass bottle off the counter and hand it to her. "Try this one. It's mine."

She narrows her eyes at me, but sniffs it. I can tell from the way she reacts that she likes it: eyes widening a little, small smile. Noncommittally, she says, "Hmm."

"For your...husband?" I venture again as she turns her back on me.

She whirls on me.

"For no one," she spits out. "I'm browsing, trying to kill time, because if I have to sit and think about my laptop for fifteen hours, I might cry. Or…have another panic attack. Which is the last thing I need. What about your hotel?"

I'd entertained the idea of going to a hotel, alone, for about one minute. But that was before I met her. And I realized that this trip has been a washout enough without me going back to a room, alone, and emptying out the mini-bar.

Plus…a lot could happen in fifteen hours.

I lean against one of the display cases and cross my arms. "Ah, Rebecca, Rebecca, Rebecca. How can I leave you, alone, here? That wouldn't be very gentlemanly of me."

I expect her to fight it, but she smiles. She lifts a bottle from the counter and says, "This one is mine."

I sniff it. Damn good choice. "You wear this? No wonder I want to lick you up and down." I lean forward. "Let me smell it on you."

She takes a step back, gives me a cautious look. "Why?"

"Because it smells different on every person."

She tilts her head to the side, baring her neck for me, as if she's welcoming the vampire's kiss. I lean in and inhale.

Fucking In. Cred. I. Ble.

And just that she lets me this close to her, close enough that I could lick that perfect, swanlike neck of hers, seals the deal.

All that protesting? It's a front. She's into this.

I place a hand on the small of her back and guide her out toward the main concourse. "If you would like to research for your book, believe it or not, there are places we can be alone. Even in this airport. The family restroom, for instance."

She lets out a bitter laugh. "Oh. That would be *really* romantic."

"It's not the place, Rebecca," I say as she looks up, licking those full pink lips of hers wet. She's begging to be kissed. "It's never the place. It's always the person."

chapter three

Becka

I'm not sure how it happens.

One moment we're standing in the airport, next to the Aunt Annie's pretzel stand. I'm innocently comparing him to Ben, my ideal man, whom he's nothing like.

The next moment, he pulls me with his strong hands toward the flat planes of his body, and his lips descend. Suddenly I'm tasting him. I can feel his hardness pressing into my body as we both taste from one another.

A little voice in the back of my head warns me to pull back—the guy is a total STRANGER. But I'm kissing him like that doesn't matter—and *does* it *even* matter? Right now all that matters are the feel of his square shoulders under my grip, the way his tongue pushes and teases mine, the way my toes are curling in a way that I write about in my book but not exactly a way that I'd ever felt before.

His tongue keeps lapping at mine, pleasure ricocheting off the walls of my body.

When we peel free, I'm gasping, and the guy growls and pulls me back to him. "Hotel room. Now. I have to have you," he demands huskily.

I want this guy. How long since I had sex? Four months ago? How long since I felt like this? Have I ever?

I look at him, suddenly annoyed that some random guy can make me lose it like this. Have me panting like this.

"Who do you think you are?"

"I'm the guy whose name you'll be screaming all over tonight."

I'm having trouble following and deciding why I let this guy maul and kiss me, but my body is burning head to toe. "I don't even know your name."

This is so freaking backwards. I kissed him even before I knew his name! I'm not sure if he reminds me of someone, a movie star, but I can't remember the movie. Which is weird, because I'm good at movies.

All I know is, Ben would never behave this way.

He romanced Leia, gradually letting the heat and passion build to a head. He didn't just barrel on in there and take what he wanted.

But the thing is? I kind of liked it.

No. Scratch that. I loved it. I'm still reeling. And I want that hotel room. Why did I say no, again?

"Noah," he breathes. He reaches out and touches a lock of my dull beige hair that's come loose from the bun. He wraps it around his finger, his cool gray eyes moving from my forehead, to my nose, to my chin. "Now you know. Hotel?"

I want him. God, I want him. I bet he can do a lot more than help with my research.

But I also can't leave my laptop. "I… I can't."

He backs off of me, still twirling a lock of my hair, a smile of mischief on his face. "Told you. Chapter three."

"Hmph," I say, looking around. We'd been making out, hot and heavy, right in front of the Hudson Newsstand with a display for motion sickness bands. That doesn't even make for a good romance novel. I flush. "I'm not one for PDAs."

"Wow. No PDAs, and your laptop means more to you than a good, toe-curling orgasm? Interesting."

Actually…it's a very close toss-up. He has no idea how close. My head is a rush and my heart is fluttering.

"I, for one, *am* into a good PDA. In fact, airports used to be a lot more romantic before nine-eleven, when they used to let just anybody up to the gates. People making out, kissing hello and goodbye. If you ask me, airports have had the romance sucked right out of them. And the least we can do is try to bring a little of it back."

Right. Please. If it doesn't have the Eiffel Tower or an Italian vineyard or a sky full of stars in it, it's not romantic. The end.

I head to the Aunt Annie's stand and pluck napkins out of the dispenser, hoping I can easily erase the pressure of his lips, the delicious way he smelled, the way his hard body felt against mine…

"Are you that wet?" He breathes on his fingernails and buffs them with the front of his t-shirt. "Don't know my own strength sometimes."

I frown at him and sit down at the nearest chair. I find a pen in my bag and hold it at the ready.

He sits beside me. So close, thigh-to-thigh. I can't bring myself to move because my body clearly loves it.

"What are you doing?" he asks.

I ignore him. Or try to, at least. I try to concentrate on the people walking by, but all I can think about is the man right next to me. The contours of his muscles under his t-shirt. The way he fills out his jeans. The way his hair tumbles over his forehead in a sort of messy way. Eyes that are the coldest gray and yet still manage to smolder.

"Nothing. Just..." I frown at the empty napkin. "I have time to kill. I need to work. Trying to come up with a character sketch for some of my side characters. They say people-watching helps."

He crosses his arms and watches as people rush by. Then he looks at my paper, waiting for me to write something.

Only I can't.

I think of the way he smells.

The way he kisses.

The way he touches me.

I can't think of a single damn thing that isn't about him.

He shifts in his seat, and I can tell he's getting impatient, waiting for me. I'm getting impatient for myself. But I refuse to call my NYC trip a total wash. Not when I have fifteen hours to kill.

"That woman over there is a first-time grandmother," he says, pointing to an older woman with curly gray hair who is clutching her ticket and staring at the departures board. "She's never travelled alone before because her husband died last month, but she desperately wants to see her new grandbaby. Her name is Mavis, she lives in Vermont, and she's travelling down to Atlanta."

I tilt my head. "Hmm. I love her Converse high-tops."

He points to the napkin on my lap, his hand resting on my thigh. Instantly, skin pebbles. Dammit. "That's a detail for your napkin."

He's right. I scribble that down.

He's good at this. Weirdly good at this. Most people don't notice details like that. Only artists. "Are you a writer, too?"

"I've written before. Nothing published." He scratches the side of his face and points across the aisle, at an Asian girl who has her nose buried in her phone. "She has a flight to Seattle to meet with someone she met on the internet."

I raise an eyebrow. "Really? What makes you think that?"

"Because one, she's sitting at the Seattle gate. Second, she's been texting like crazy since she sat down, and looking around like she's up to no good. I bet she's sending dirty messages."

I eye the girl. She looks so straight-laced. "Please."

"Also, she's too dressed up for a six-hour flight. She's definitely up to no good."

I write down a few details about her. *Short skirt, dark glasses, shiny raven hair...dating someone she met online?* Then I snap a picture of her with my phone.

He's leaning close to me, looking at my notes. God, he smells delicious.

"You have to go deeper than that. Why don't you try?" He points out a man who's walking down the hall at a furious pace, constantly looking over his shoulder. He's a middle-aged man with a full beard and a tweed blazer, clutching a beaten leather bag under his arm.

"He...looks like a criminal. Or a serial killer."

The corners of his mouth turn up. "Something real."

I throw up my hands. "That *is* real! I don't know! He looks guilty. Shifty. That's all."

"You're a very suspicious person, did anyone ever tell you that?"

I point emphatically. "Look. At. Him. Tell me I'm wrong. That guy has Maximum Security written all over his face."

He strokes the stubble on his chin. "He looks like a professor who's nervous about missing his flight. Or a writer." He nods seriously at me. "Writers are weird. Paranoid. I met one once."

I elbow him in the ribs. "I don't know. I feel like I've seen him before..." I sigh. "Either I'm tired, or I'm going crazy."

"Probably a little of both. Why?"

"I'm having déjà vu all over the place. First you, and now him. I really feel like I've seen you both before."

He clears his throat. "Well, I'd remember if I'd seen *you* before."

I tap my finger on my mouth as I study him. His kind of gorgeousness should be outlawed. I should know where I've seen him before. "You do look familiar, but I can't place it."

He looks away, drains the rest of his coffee. "So tell me more about Ben and Leia."

He really seems interested, and maybe it's just that he wants in my pants. But I don't care. Maybe talking out my plot dilemma will help me figure out the ending. "Well, Ben's a billionaire, and Leia is an awkward college student. Their meet-cute is at a Starbucks in the city where she's a barista, and they—"

"Meet-cute? What's that?"

"You know. When they meet and sparks fly. You see, she makes him a latte and he ordered a black coffee, and—"

"A Starbucks? That sounds dull. What about an airport?"

"Airport? No."

"Why?"

"Because airports are usually places of frustration and stress. In a Starbucks, everyone's happy, drinking their coffees, relaxing. It's a perfect place for a meet-cute."

"I think we proved that airports *can* be romantic."

I shake my head. "Starbucks. It's cute because she makes the wrong drink, then puts her number on the coffee cup before she hands it to him, and then he calls her, and…it's perfect."

I smile, proud of myself.

"Sounds…interesting." He says "interesting" in a tone that sounds like *the most boring idea I've ever heard.* "Let me guess. Their first kiss is in front of the Eiffel Tower?"

I frown. How can I simultaneously hate and want someone so much?

"Really? I'm right?" He even seems surprised.

I stiffen. Yes, he is, but there's no way I'm telling him that. Suddenly my brilliant idea seems so banal. So…boring.

He lifts a finger like he's just had a brainstorm. "Wait. What about two people who miss the same flight? They go back to a hotel and have a night of unbridled—"

"Stoooop," I mutter. "Stop with the airport, already. It's never happening."

He holds up his hands in surrender. Then he takes out his phone and starts thumbing away. I look over his shoulder and see him thumbing stuff into the notepad on his phone.

I shouldn't care. But I do.

"What are you doing?"

He shrugs. "I'm writing my own book."

I roll my eyes. I hate how everyone and their mother thinks they can write a book. As if it doesn't take any talent whatsoever. But I'm also…intrigued. "About…"

I try to peek, but he shields it from my view. His eyes settle on me, totally *unsettling* me. "I think you know."

My jaw drops. I pluck the phone out of his hand and read:

Her name was Rebecca. I met her when we both missed the 5:15 pm out of JFK. I was headed to L.A. But the second I touched her, I knew our lives would never be the

My face heats.

He might be onto something.

Damn him.

I suck in a breath. "Are…you from L.A.?"

He nods and snatches the phone back. "Hands off, woman. It's my idea now."

I cross my arms and ball the napkin in my fist. I don't know why I never thought about putting notes in my phone. Oh, right. Because up until now my laptop had been more attached to me than my own limbs.

"I'll be nice and let you help me with my research, though," he says, dropping a hand on my thigh.

He moves it in slow circles and…it feels nice. Instantly, I would love to help him research anything he'd like.

And he knows it. He drags his hand down past the hem of my skirt, to my bare knee.

And oh, my god. What would Bryn say if I told her that I actually entertained fucking a guy I absolutely will never see again? Probably that it's been way too long since Trevor, and I need to stop living in my head and get out more.

Who am I kidding? Bryn would probably break out the pom-poms.

But come on. The last thing I need is a one-night-stand with a guy that'll leave me feeling just as lonely as I have for the past four months. Texas is big. It should not be this hard to find someone who actually lives in my state. Someone who is not Trevor.

Just then, a teenaged girl walks past us with a slice of pizza.

"Hey," I say. "I haven't eaten since breakfast. You want to get something to eat?"

chapter four

Noah

We're sitting at the bar in a place called Bobby Van's Steakhouse, side-by-side, perusing the same menu as some hockey game blares overhead.

I know what I want, but it's not on the menu. I'm close to her because she smells great and her cleavage is right there, close enough to bury my face in.

I've never been into hockey, but the two guys next to me, who are obviously drunk, keep screaming at the screen.

Rebecca rolls her eyes.

"I take it you're not a hockey fan."

"In my family, if it's not played with a football, it's not a sport," she says. "What about you?"

I shrug. "I'm not a sports fan, period."

"Wow, a guy who doesn't like sports? What happened to you? Were you dropped on your head as a child?"

I grin and call the bartender over. "Corona," I tell him and look at her.

"Um. I guess I'll take a Corona, too." She studies the menu and gnaws on her lip, tucking a loose strand of blonde hair behind her ear. "And…chicken nachos."

I nod at the bartender. "Nachos. We'll share." I look at her. "Unless you want them all to yourself?"

"I'll give you some…maybe." She wiggles her eyebrows mysteriously. "So, what do you do in L.A.? Are you in the movie business?"

I nod. "Indeed I am."

She raises an eyebrow. "You're an actor?"

"Yep."

"Really? Have I seen you in anything?" Her jaw drops. "I must have! That's why you look so familiar!"

I shrug. "Possible. Do you watch a lot of movies?"

"Oh my god, I'm addicted to the movies. Seriously. Romantic comedies, dramas, thrillers, fantasies…all of it." She stops abruptly. "Oh. Except super-hero movies. Why are there so many super-hero movies coming out these days? I'd rather watch paint dry. Seriously."

I stop myself before the laugh escapes my throat. "You probably haven't seen me in anything. I was in a couple indie flicks a few years back that nobody's heard of."

"Really? Which ones?"

"The first one was called *Going Home.* I was twenty. It was a—"

"Get out." Her mouth is hanging open. "I saw that when I was in high school and it was my favorite movie ever. Oh, my god. That's you. You're Brock, the drug-addicted baseball player."

I nod. "Guilty as charged."

She covers her face with her hands. "Oh my god. I love you. You're brilliant. You're like, a real, actual talent."

I wonder what she'd think if she knew I sold out to become a giant stone man in a loincloth who shows no emotion on the screen whatsoever and says fewer than three words per movie. "Thanks."

"I—I can't believe this!" She reaches into the console in front of us and pulls out a napkin. "Can you sign this?"

I haven't signed an autograph since the last press junket for *The Galaxy Survives* at Comic-Con, last summer. I scribble my name on the napkin, right above the Ben's logo, and she holds it to her heart. I'm suddenly jealous of that napkin.

She reads it. "Noah Steele. Of course. Noah Steele!"

I give her a serious look. "Are you rethinking the hotel, now that you know I'm a big movie star?"

She rolls her eyes. "No. But wow. I have to text my sister this." She pushes the napkin into her bag and grabs her phone. "We actually quote that movie to each other on a daily basis. You know the part where you say to Cassie, your girlfriend, 'Even if you don't got your bases full, going home is still damn sweet'? Swoon! That's like our favorite line!"

"Yep. I know that line."

"Or…or…when the coach wants you off the team?" She frowns, lowers her voice an octave, and mutters, "'You don't give up when the thing you love hangs in the balance. You dig deeper. You taught me that, coach.'"

I'm amused by the inflection in her voice. She almost sounds like me. She may also be the only person I've ever met who ever quoted me back to me. "Yeah. Profound."

She starts thumbing in that text. "She'll never believe this."

"Want to send a selfie with me as evidence?"

Her face lights up. "Yes! Would you mind?"

I shake my head. I take my hat off and run my hand through my hair. I twine my arm around her small waist, my hand on her hip. Fuck, she smells like candy, and when I press my cheek against hers for the pose, her skin is as soft as rose petals. It incites a riot inside me, every one of my senses demanding more.

But she snaps the picture and quickly pulls away. She presses send and grins at the picture of us. "Oh, my god. She'll freak. So what are you doing lately? Why were you in New York?"

"Auditioning for a Broadway production of Hamlet, actually," I mumble, my spirits sinking. "Waste of time."

"They didn't like your audition?"

I shake my head. "That's an understatement." *Apparently, Hamlet is not pretty or buff.* "But I have plenty of irons in the fire. Just a matter of being in the right place at the right time."

"Aw. You're a starving artist like me, then, huh?" She moves in close to me, her hair falling on my shoulder. "I mean, I'm not exactly starving. But until I get my big break with my book, it's just…nose to the grindstone, you know?"

I smile, though I can't say I think of Megalith as my "art."

Our beers come, and I dunk the lime and take a swig. "Or until you meet that billionaire of yours."

She's confused. "What?"

"The book. You're Leia. And your ideal man is Ben. Filthy rich. Right?"

She pushes the lime into the neck of her beer. "Well. I'm not going to lie. Money's nice. But it's not everything. It just makes things more romantic. They jet-set off to Paris for their first date, and make love in his private penthouse deck, with the New York City skyline beneath them. Can't really do that when you're poor."

"Yeah. But you can do better things."

She gives me a doubtful look. "Like?"

"Family restroom at the airport."

She looks away, but I catch the way her pulse thrums in her throat. "Yeah. Hmm. That's a close rival to Paris. I mean, I know what you said. It's never the place, it's the person. But sometimes, you have to admit, the setting really does help."

"Ok. Fine. You know what? I think you are the reason why women have unrealistic expectations when they date. Really. Would you want a man to just whisk you off, last minute, to Paris?"

She doesn't even skip a beat. "Hell yes. It's every woman's fantasy."

"So you'd like to take a fourteen-hour roundtrip flight for a date that would be…what? Three hours, tops?"

She frowns. "Well, no, but it's still romantic. My best friend—"

"Nobody really writes romances featuring a starving artist as the male lead, do they? They don't fit the mold."

"I…guess not." She stares at her beer and her eyes widen. "Oh, my god. Why do I keep babbling on to you about my book like this? I usually hate talking about my books. My best friend and sister are the only ones who know I'm writing this one."

"Yeah? Why's that?"

"Because every time I tell people I'm a writer, they ask if they might have read anything I've written. And I always say no because I'm not published yet, which is really embarrassing." She freezes. "Oh. God. I just realized that's what I did to you. I asked if I'd seen anything you've been in. You probably get that all the time."

She's my undoing, the way she looks up at me with that girlish innocence. "Yeah. But I don't care. If I don't like the person who's asking, I usually end up listing titles that sound like potential porno flicks. It usually shuts them up."

She laughs. "Hmm. So I should tell them I wrote the novelization of Debbie Does Dallas?" She taps her chin thoughtfully. "Could work."

Her face turns somber, and she gives me a smile that makes me want to get deep inside her and unravel every one of those storylines she has in her head.

"I guess the truth is…after this, you're going to L.A. I'm going to Austin. We're never going to see each other again. So…"

"Hotel?" I suggest.

She takes a ladylike sip of her beer, really good at ignoring me now. "I'll let you read my first chapter, when I have my laptop back."

I want that. I want to see what kind of hot things are going through this sweet little girl's mind. "You're on."

She brings her thumbnail to her mouth, gnawing on it. "I'm just thinking. I never talk to anyone about my creative process. That must be why I'm talking to you about mine."

I lay a finger on her forearm, and the hairs stand on end. "Or it might be that same irresistible connection that has your skin doing this, every time we touch."

She looks up at me, her hair falling in her face, and licks her lips.

She wants me. And I want her.

But we only have twelve hours left.

The waiter slides a massive plate of nachos over to us, along with two small appetizer plates. She hands one to me and takes a massive helping of them, dripping with cheese, onto her plate.

As she chews, she punches in a call. She says, "Hello, I'm calling for status on a laptop I reported missing…yes, thank you…okay…thanks anyway." She hangs up and frowns.

I pop an olive into my mouth and frown. "You're persistent, you know that?"

"You think it's gone?"

I hate to admit it, but yeah. I nod.

She sighs. "You're probably right."

I can see how much it means to her. She looks just about as lost as I did when I left the audition this afternoon. And like Brock says in *Going Home,* you don't give up when the thing you love hangs in the balance. You dig deeper.

"Doesn't mean you shouldn't look for it. We can scour the place." I turn my chair toward her. "How about this? I take Concourse B, you take C. Then we'll meet back here in an hour?"

Her eyes light up. "That would be great. Thanks."

chapter five

Becka

An hour after I set out to find my laptop, I'm sitting at the same bar where I ate my nachos, on my third beer, and thinking of asking for something stronger.

No laptop.

That's it. My life is over.

I pick up my phone, desperate for a text from Lily. The girl's so focused, she usually turns off her phone whenever she's studying for a big exam. I guess that pesky little bar exam qualifies.

Instead I see a text from Bryn. ***You get home all right?***

Me: ***I missed my flight. Still at JFK.***

Bryn: ***!!! Why didn't you text me?***

That's the last thing I'd do. She and Christos are not only together again, they just got engaged. Me moping around complaining about my pathetic life wouldn't exactly be a nice engagement gift.

Me: ***I lost my laptop somewhere in the wilds of the airport and I'm not leaving until I find it.***

Bryn: ***OMG!! Are you serious? Are you ok?***

Me: ***After I got over the heart palpitations.***

Bryn: ***Poor baby! Are you sure you don't want me to come get you?***

Me: ***I'm sure, bestie. I may have met someone.***

Bryn: ***True story? In the airport? Dish, pls!!***

Me: ***Don't get too excited. As far as relationships go, it's extremely short-term. He lives in L.A.***

Bryn: ***Hot actor???***

Me: ***Bingo. He was like in my favorite movie EVER***

Bryn: ***OMG! Which one?***

Me: ***He played Brock in Going Home***

Bryn: ***Never heard of it. Or wait. Wasn't that a kid's movie? About pets who lose their owners and have to find them?***

Me: ***NOOO***

Bryn: ***I just looked him up on IMDB. Noah Steele? Holy crap he's hot, baby girl! Those eyes!!! Jump him!***

Me: ***That thought has only occurred to me like, once a second since I met him. AND he wanted me to get a hotel room with him.***

Bryn: ***That's hotttt. So what if it's a one-night-stand? Ride him cowgirl! Fuel your creativity!!! I need to know what happens with Ben and Leia!***

Me: ***I can't think creatively when my laptop is in someone else's hands!***

Bryn: ***All right, then just get a good O. A good O makes everything better!***

Me: ***I'm thinking about it…***

"Hey."

I straighten, trying to stop my heart from beating out of my chest as he slides onto the stool next to me.

Brock. I spent many a day in high school fantasizing about this man. Right now, my fifteen-year-old self is doing cartwheels. My twenty-five-year-old self?

Is doing cartwheels—internally—but also wants her damn laptop back.

I lower my eyes to his hands. Strong, manly hands that I can picture on the curves of my body. No hot-pink laptop.

He does, however, have a small pack of butter rum Life Savers, which he rolls on the bar over to me.

That, and his apologetic look, are my consolation prizes.

He motions the bartender. "Another round."

"No," I say, too loud. "Another round, and a shot of Fireball."

"Make that two."

I smile up at him, ruefully. I am fully prepared to drink my ass off tonight.

The bartender sets the shots of amber liquid in front of us. He raises his to make a toast but I down mine before he can say a word. When I look up at him, he has a surprised look on his face.

"I'm from Texas. Drinking is our national pastime," I explain, motioning to the bartender. "Another."

He shifts in his seat to face me, leaning against the back of the stool, legs spread as if he owns the place, powerful and relaxed. "Well, that's better than where I'm from. In Hollywood, we just do a lot of cocaine."

I laugh miserably.

We match each other, shot for shot, until everything around me gets bleary.

Everything, that is, except him.

No, the pleasant buzziness inside me has me hyper-focused on him, with his disheveled hair and darkening sandy stubble on his strong jaw. I gaze at the muscles stretching and flexing under his t-shirt as he rests his arms on the bar. His biceps and forearms, tanned and strong, make me weak.

I go back to my beer. Somehow, we end up drawing pictures of people in the bar on napkins. Drunk and completely unartistic, my efforts end up being pretty messy. It's a good thing no one else sees them or I'd probably get beaten up. He's a much better artist than I am.

"So," I ask him as I sketch. "You wanted to be on Broadway?"

"Yeah, I mean. I was on Broadway. I got my start in acting when I was twelve. A peanut butter commercial."

I laugh. "Seriously?"

"Yep. Supposedly I have a face that sells shit. After that my parents kept shipping me up to New York for auditions. Small parts, mostly. I was in Les Mis on Broadway the year before I went to college. One of the revolutionaries. Then in college, I played pretty much all the male leads. In attendance one night was a producer looking for someone who could be in his semi-autobiographical movie about a baseball player struggling with heroin addiction, and the rest is history."

"That's so cool," I say, half-gushing, so close to drooling it's not even funny. "I guess it is all about being in the right place at the right time. Because I can't imagine anyone else playing Brock. What was this play you were trying out for?"

"It was a modernized, musical version of Hamlet. I was pretty psyched about it. But apparently I'm too hot to be their Hamlet." He shrugs matter-of-factly. I get the feeling he is very used to being called gorgeous, because it's an undeniable fact. Yet another reason I can't believe he's wasting time with me. "But that's the business. There's a revival of *Rent* coming up that I might be in the running for."

"*Rent*?"

"Yeah. You ever seen it? The part of Roger."

"Oh. You mean, the one who sings, *One Song Glory?*" When he nods, I feel a sinking in my stomach. "So…you can sing, then?"

He nods.

"Are you good?"

"Capable."

"I didn't know Brock could sing. Can you…sing for me?"

His eyes scan me predatorily, and a small smile curls his lips. "Right here?" He narrows his eyes at me like I'm a nutbag. Which I am. And he's kind of flustering me right now, as hot as he is. I think if a song ever burst from his pretty perfect lips, I'd probably have an orgasm right there.

And I bet he can probably dance, too.

My voice can burst eardrums. And he would hate to see my uncoordinated bovine ass on the dance floor.

He's a much better *everything* than I am.

I bet he's an amazing lover. I bet he fucks just as well as he kisses—hot and hard and full of raw passion.

The more I drink, the more I wonder why I turned him down.

Oh, right…because I have an uncoordinated bovine ass and if I ever hopped into bed with him, he'd know it.

We decide to do portraits of each other. I get to really look at him. Sandy hair that's longer than Brock's was, tumbling over his tan skin. A dimple in the center of his chin that I just want to lick. Stubble like stardust. He's better looking now than in *Going Home.* Back then he was only a teenager. Now, he's more mature. More muscles, definitely. He's grown into himself.

He can definitely inspire me.

He sits at the table, closing his eyes and pressing at his temples. "Do you have a headache, too?" I ask him.

"No. Just waiting for my bitch muse to come into play."

Then he claps his hands, hunches over his napkin, a contemplative look in his eyes like Leo gave Kate during that scene in *Titanic,* as he sets in to sketch me.

God, I'm wet. The place between my thighs is so tingly, it's practically humming.

I feel myself loosening up, laughing harder, wondering why the fuck I cared so much about my laptop anyway.

"And…one, two, three…now!"

We both slap our pictures on the bar, the final reveal. I wound up drawing a picture of him that makes him look like Popeye. Just need the corn-cob pipe. His picture of me? Beautiful. Should be in a museum somewhere. He used maybe twelve strokes total, and I can see a slight resemblance, though the girl in the picture is much too sexy-looking to be me.

Apparently, his muse *isn't* such a bitch, and has blessed him mightily.

"Sorry," I say, slumping over the bar. "I'm terrible."

"Don't be," he says, studying the picture seriously. He puts a finger under my chin, lifting my face so I have no choice but to stare, not at him, but at the butt-ugly picture I drew. "Look at it. I'm flattered you think so much of me with those muscles. I, on the other hand, didn't do you justice."

I can barely talk. Just his finger on my chin is enough to make me pant. And no, he doesn't have bulging Popeye muscles, but what he does have? *Way* better. Enough to get the corners of my mouth glistening with drool.

Unaware, he lifts his ass off the stool, pockets the picture in the back of his jeans, and checks his phone. "Eleven more hours."

I spin on the stool, away from the bar. It's well after midnight and the airport traffic has definitely calmed from the frenetic craziness of earlier. Now, there are only a few people, milling about, waiting for their red-eyes. It's almost somber now.

Quiet. And he's probably the hottest thing these airport walls have ever seen. Brock. The real. Freaking. Brock. I've been creeping my ass closer to him on the stool for the past two hours, wanting to touch him, wanting my skin to light up the way he always seems to make it do. The social lubrication is only fueling the desire.

I want to stand up, steal my hands up that tight gray t-shirt of his, feeling the muscles underneath. I want to kiss him like we did before, but I don't want to stop there.

"What do you want to do now?" I ask, leaning on the bar, giving him my sexiest pout, trying to look as much as I can like the girl he drew in the picture.

He gives me a lazy-sexy look, those gray eyes penetrating right to my core. "We'll think of something."

Now he's looking at my mouth, contemplating it, so I flick my tongue out, slowly wetting my bottom lip. Preparing for the kiss, if you will.

Suddenly he claps his hands. "What about a scavenger hunt?"

Um. That was so not what I was thinking. "Huh?"

He hooks a finger toward me. "Give me your phone."

"Uh…"

I hand it to him, reluctant because I'm worried he might see the conversation I'd had with Bryn, which may have included something about jumping and riding him.

He lays his phone in my lap, his fingers brushing my thigh, lingering there.

"Here are the rules. Write down ten things that I have to find or take a picture of within the confines of this terminal. It can be anything, but it has to be something that can be located within this terminal. Nothing like a volcano, or a real dinosaur, or whatever. Got it?"

I nod. "Okay. I guess." Not really. Because right now, I want to be near him. Not scampering all over God's creation looking for things. "What are we playing for?"

"Well, whoever gets their items first, wins." He scratches his chin. "The other person has to grant the winner one wish."

I narrow my eyes at him. "One wish?"

His lips curve in a devilish way that makes my heart thump. "Anything they want."

"Anything?"

"So if you don't want to lose, you'd better put some damn good things on your list." He's full-on grinning at me, wolfishly, like he's going to eat me for dinner.

And he's so got me beat. I can't even think of my own name when he looks at me like that.

I open up his phone and try to concentrate. At first I'm totally blank, only aware of the total hotness of him, next to me. Then I get down to business and start churning out some decent ideas.

I smile when I'm done and hand him his phone. He texts me, so now we can text each other pictures of the things we find. "Do we have a time limit?"

He signals to the bartender for the check, then takes his wallet out of his back pocket and lays it on the counter between us. "Nah. Whoever gets them all first."

"And if no one does?"

"Then no one gets their wish."

I slide off the stool. "Deal."

I reach over and shake his hand, and even numb as hell, I feel my skin electrify in a way it never has before.

The check comes across the bar, and he lifts it, setting a credit card down. The bartender takes it away.

"I could've split that."

"It's the least I can do. Since you're in for total defeat." He leans in. How the hell does he smell so good? His breath warm on my ear. "I bet you can guess what my wish is."

And he pockets his credit card, spins and heads off, checking his phone as he strides confidently away.

Maybe it's the Fireball.

But right now, *I'm* the Fireball.

It probably is a good idea to get away from him. Maybe then, I can cool my sorry, overheated ass down.

chapter six

Noah

I leave the bar with only one thing on my mind.

Winning this game.

I know, the hotel idea is looking bleaker by the moment. It's one in the morning. We only have slightly over ten hours left.

But I'm not giving up. I'm digging deep.

Brock would be proud. Megalith, however, is letting out his subhuman growl, flexing his muscles, wondering why the hell I want to distance myself from him.

Because… Rebecca.

The more I know her, the more I want to run from that big blue asshole. The more I think there was something else I was put on this earth to do, and that I just need to channel my muse, get her to behave, and let her show me my destiny.

I stare at my phone screen, at the list of items she'd put in.

The first one: ***The arrivals screen***

I laugh at that. Is she serious? Or does she just want me that bad?

I go to the wall of the concourse, not twenty paces from the front of the restaurant, and snap a picture. Then I text it to her, with the words, ***You're going down.***

Or I might go down on her. Yes, I would like that very much.

All right. Head in the game. Don't get too far ahead of yourself, Steele.

Number two on the list: ***Splenda packets***

I grin. I really thought a writer would be more creative than this. She clearly needs help in freeing her creative inhibitions. And other inhibitions, as well. I could help with that, if she'd just let me.

I cruise on over to the nearest restaurant, which happens to be Bobby Van's, the one I just left, as my phone lights up with a text from her. It says, ***Clever girl.***

Okay. Not a superhero movie fan, but a *Jurassic Park* fan? Interesting.

I head over to the hostess and ask her if she has any packets of Splenda. She nods, heads into the back, and returns a moment later with a handful of them.

I snap a picture and tell her she can take them back, much to her confusion and annoyance.

As I'm about to text the picture to Rebecca, I look up and see her.

She's still sitting at the bar. A full beer in front of her. Shoulders slumped.

I don't think she got the point of this hunt. Either that, or she's really devastated about that laptop. I can't help but feel bad for her.

I text her the picture, then sidle up behind her, leaning over her shoulder. God, she smells good. “Hey,” I say. “Forfeiting already? All right. I accept your surrender, although you will have to submit to my terms.”

She takes a swig of her beer. Renegade hair from her bun falls in her bleary eyes. She may be drunk, or nearly there.

“Submit nothing,” she mumbles. “I’ve got this.”

I point to her phone. “I’m still on top. Which is where I’ll be when you *do* submit.”

She gives me a surly smile, leaning forward so close she nearly falls off the bar stool. “Don’t be so sure, Mr. Egocentric Movie Star,” she says, beeping me on the nose.

“Whoa.” She is drunk. Fuck. All right. I push the beer away from her and motion to the bartender. “Can we get a glass of water here?”

She frowns at me. “I’m fine.”

“Okay. I know.”

She shoves me away. “I am! It’s just…” She sighs. “I don’t know. I know it means nothing to you. You have a billion talents to fall back on, Mr. Singer-slash-Dancer-slash-Actor-slash-Artist person. But the only thing I’ve ever been even remotely good at is writing.”

I sit next to her as the water comes. I reach into my carry-on and pull out a container of Excedrin. I pop two on the napkin next to the glass. “I’m sure that’s not true.”

“It is. Lily was always the smart one. Bryn was always the ambitious one.”

“Your sisters?”

“Lily’s my younger sister. Bryn’s my best friend. Growing up, we were like the Three Musketeers. They were always so focused. They went out and got what they wanted. But what was I? The dreamer," she mutters miserably. "Most likely to fall in a hole while walking down the street because her head's not just in the clouds, it's in another universe entirely."

Her shoulders slump farther. She takes a pill, swallows it, and sips the water.

"So when I say that laptop is my life… I mean, it's my life. My self-worth is all wrapped up in that stupid contraption. And I just went and…lost it. How could I have been so stupid?"

This is a drunken rant if ever I heard one. "Hey. Look at me."

She does. There are tears in her eyes.

I plant my hands on her shoulders. They're graceful and thin and as I press my fingertips through, massaging the contours and angles, I don't want to stop there. "You're from Texas, right? Everything is bigger in Texas, right? Your ego… your will…"

"My ass?"

"You have a perfect ass. Trust me," I tell her. "What I'm saying is that Texas girls don't quit. You don't let this drag you down."

She eyes me doubtfully. "How do you know what Texas girls do?"

"What makes you worthwhile is not in that computer." I tap the side of her head. "It's in here."

She sniffles. I can tell she doesn't believe me.

"Got it, Texas?"

Her lower lip quivers, and she sucks it in to stop it. It's the most seductive thing I've ever seen.

I pull her into a hug. Kiss the top of her head. "Hey. It's all right."

She relaxes against me. God, she feels perfect in my arms.

But it lasts only a fraction of a second. She straightens, grabs a napkin off the bar, and blows her nose.

"Yeah. I'm good." It's like someone flipped a switch. She slides her phone off the bar and opens it. "Scavenger hunt. I'm ready to kick some ass."

"You sure you want to—"

"Hell, yes."

I give her a doubtful look. I'm not sure I want to win now, kick her while she's down. I take out my wallet and lay a ten down on the table for her beer, as she begins gathering her things off the bar. "Because just a second ago, you looked like—"

"No. Bring it. I'm going to clean the floor with your ass."

For someone with all of her self-worth tied to a stupid contraption, she's pretty big on trash talk. I give her a grin. "That so? I think I happen to be way ahead."

"Not for long." She slides off the seat, takes a sip of her water, and whatever drunken stupor I'd thought she was in before seems to disappear. "You think I was hanging out here because I wasn't into the game?"

I stare at her.

She winks at me and leans in, whispering, just as confidently as I had earlier, "I was giving you a head start. I thought you'd need it."

Then she gives me a wave and skips into a run.

What. The…?

I think I've been had.

I walk out onto the concourse, smiling and checking the next item on the list. ***The I <3 NY logo.***

Easier than taking candy from a baby.

Just then, a text comes in from Rebecca. It's a picture. I open it to see a selfie of her, cheek-to-cheek, with a woman with shocking red hair and a number of piercings in her lips, nose, eyebrow, cheek and tongue. They actually both have their tongues out, wagging at me.

She's got my number one: ***Someone with an unusual piercing.***

So she's gaining on me.

And it's clear she's brought her A game.

No more feeling sorry for her.

Game on.

I head over to the nearest gift shop on the concourse, which happens to be the Hudson News where we first kissed. There's a display of t-shirts, teddy bears, hats, and other things with the familiar logo.

As I'm snapping a photo, another picture comes through.

I glance at it. It's the number two from my list: ***A pilot with a beard.***

Shit. We're tied.

Then I read the message she wrote underneath: ***#2 and #7. Suck it.***

Number seven? I can't…

It hits me right then. Number seven was: ***Someone named Sidney.***

I look back at the picture. Sure enough, he's pointed at the name badge on his lapel, which says Sidney Loftin.

Son of a bitch. Of all the luck.

She's ahead of me.

I quickly text her back my picture to even up the score.

I may have underestimated her.

It occurs to me then that she's skipping ahead. Which, dammit, makes sense. Taking things one at a time wasn't in the rules. So I scroll through the rest of her list.

And fuck me.

It gets harder.

Like she was sliding into her groove. Or she wanted to lure me into a false sense of security.

But that's fine. I'll win this. I've got my number ten. She'll never be able to find my number ten.

My number four is ***Mary Anne Evans.***

I let out a sigh and look around. Yeah, I guess one of these people could be named Mary Anne Evans, but it would be a fucking long shot. And I don't think I'll be as lucky as she was with her Sidney.

I go to the first podium I can find. The attendant looks up.

"Hi. I'm traveling with someone and I think I've lost her. Can you page her for me?"

She nods and picks up her phone. "Name?"

"Mary Anne Evans."

She presses a button, and as she starts to speak, the words sound overhead. "Mary Anne Evans. Paging Mary Anne Evans. Please meet your party at Gate 12."

"Thanks," I tell her, as my phone buzzes with another text.

I look. It's a picture of her posing with a security guard and his pooch. She's got my number six. ***Drug-sniffing dog.***

Shit, shit, shit. She's ahead of me now. Only six more to go. I made it way too easy.

No. I've still got my number ten. She'll never get my number ten.

At least, I think.

I scan the airport, waiting for my Mary Anne Evans to arrive and save me like Sidney the Pilot saved Rebecca. Of course, it's not happening. But goddammit, she's right. I'm sure many people named Mary Anne Evans could feasibly have walked through this terminal.

She just isn't here now.

Fuck me.

I'm going to lose this.

Just then, Rebecca practically skips past me, holding her phone and swinging her carry-on. She's with the pierced girl from her first picture, who from the way they look like two peas in a pod, must now be her partner in crime. She's making friends, kicking ass, and taking names. "Hey, Brock! What, did Mary Anne stand you up?"

I nod a stiff greeting at her. "Hello, Texas."

She hurries off, and all I can do is stare after her. Wanting to be sucked into the chasm of sensation that is her skin against mine. Wanting to see her hair spread out loose on the pillow as I thrust into her. Wanting to feel her tremble under me as we move together.

I want it so bad I can taste it.

Fuck that. I'm not losing.

No. I'm Brock. I'm digging deeper.

It's after three in the morning, and I've never felt so wired. Something is pumping through my veins. I guess you could call me competitive, but it's more than that.

I need her.

I need to be with this woman, in a way I've never needed anything.

Raking both hands through my hair, I turn to the attendant. "If Mary Anne Evans shows up, can you tell her I'll be back in a second?"

She nods.

I run down the rest of the list, thinking the rest is doable:

5. ***A person wearing an animal-shaped neck pillow***

6. ***Paisley luggage***

7. ***A Texas driver's license***

8. ***Someone famous (not you!)***

9. ***Someone really sunburned from vacation***

All right. Not a problem. I can get this done. If I can just get this Mary Anne Evans person, I'll have it made.

But then I scroll down to her number ten.

She's listed it with a smiley face, and a little note that says, ***If you can find this one, don't worry about the others… you win! Good luck*** ☺

Fuck. Me.

10. ***MacAir in a hot pink travel case***

I glance up and around for her. Somewhere, in this terminal, she must be laughing at me.

Well played, Texas. Well played.

chapter seven

Becka

My skin prickles as I nearly tackle the middle-aged couple sitting in front of a gate, waiting for their flight to Orlando.

"Excuse me," I say politely. "I notice you're wearing that crown with a veil, ma'am. Are you two newlyweds?"

She beams and nods, looking back at her husband. "We got married Saturday in Vermont. Heading to Disney for our honeymoon."

Yes!

That's just what I wanted to hear.

"Congratulations!" I say to them. "Can I ask you a favor? Can I take a picture of you? I'm doing a scavenger hunt, and honeymooners is number eight."

The woman lowers her paperback and says, "Sure."

"Thank you!" They smile for me. I snap the picture and grin at them. "Thanks again. You have no idea how much this means to me."

I quickly text it off to Noah and run over to where Robin's waiting for me.

"Good idea, finding an Orlando gate!" I tell her. "Disney *is* a top honeymoon destination."

Robin is the girl with all the piercings from my first scavenger hunt item. She's pretty cool and is on a layover from a solo trip she took to Spain, waiting to catch a flight to Omaha.

She's also just as invested in this scavenger hunt as I am.

"So. Let me get this straight," she says, pointing back down the concourse, where we'd last seen Noah. "If you win the scavenger hunt, that guy has to do anything you ask of him. But if he wins the scavenger hunt, you have to spend the night with him?"

"Mmm hmm." I'm already scanning for the remaining items on my list. Halfway there. And I'm ahead by one.

"In what way will this ever be a losing situation for you?"

I let out an uneasy laugh. "I know, I know. He's gorgeous."

"Hell girl. Sunsets are gorgeous. That man there is perfection." She gnaws on her lip ring. "So what would you ask him to do, if you win?"

"I'm still thinking."

In fact, I haven't *stopped* thinking.

"And? What are you thinking?"

"Okay, okay. He's a struggling actor, you see, looking for his next big part. And so if I win, I thought I'd ask him for tickets to his movie premiere, if he ever gets to star in a big-shot Hollywood movie, or if he ever gets on Broadway, tickets to the opening performance."

I nod with certainty as I say it. It just makes so much sense. Originally, I'd thought about asking him to meet me again. Or for that hotel room. But those sounded… I don't know…like I was forcing something that had no chance of happening. This? It's not too forward, or desperate, or perverted. And Lily and I have always talked about going to Hollywood and walking the red carpet. She'd freak.

Robin is just staring at me like I lost the top part of my head. "You're serious?"

I shrug. "You have a better idea?"

"Yeah. What *he* wants."

I squint at her. "Okay. But if we both want the same thing, then it's not a game anymore. We should just go and do it. Besides, I'm never going to see him again."

"And?"

And… I don't know. I don't want to jump into something I'll regret because it isn't a perfect love story with hearts and flowers. I guess it just doesn't seem very Ben and Leia like, for me to fuck a guy who I know I have absolutely no chance of seeing again.

No matter how sweet he is. No matter how hot he makes me.

She's waiting for an answer.

I don't have one.

Except, *And... I'm probably an idiot who will wind up missing this opportunity and regretting it my entire life.*

So I guess it all comes down to which kind of regret I can live with.

But I can't think of that now.

I deflect by pointing to my phone. "This one is hard. Where are we going to find triplets?"

She motions to me. "I think I saw some blonde kids who looked similar in age at my gate for Omaha. They could be triplets."

"Let's go."

We race toward the Omaha gate, and meanwhile I'm keeping an eye out for another set of triplets, just in case. As we run, Robin says, "What else do you need to get?"

"Um. Once we find the triplets, I just need four more. Someone in full military uniform, a green coffee stirrer, a man in a cowboy hat, and…the shark's tooth."

She slows to a stop before we reach the gate. "Wait. A shark's tooth?"

I nod. "That's what it says."

"Like…in *Jaws*? That kind of shark?"

"Um. What other kind of shark is there?"

"What the hell… That's random. How are you going to find that?"

I shrug. "Maybe in the gift shop?"

"Why? Maybe a pendant?"

I shrug. "I actually think I should challenge it. Because he said things that could be found in the airport. And I don't see how a shark's tooth can be found anywhere near JFK airport."

"Right? It's unjust!" She motions toward the couple with their three children. "I'll go ask them if they're triplets. You want to check out that gift shop for shark teeth?"

"Thanks. I guess."

I walk into the nearest Hudson News and look around. There are plenty of mementos for New York City, and even some for the Jersey Shore. But not one of them has anything resembling a shark's tooth. I know some people wear them as jewelry, so even check out the bead and hemp jewelry at the counter, but there's nothing. I ask the lady behind the counter if she knows of anything, but she shakes her head.

Totally not fair, Brock.

Although, I have to admit, what I did wasn't very fair, either.

Still, I don't like to lose.

But I might just.

Or we'll both lose.

Somehow, that makes me feel even more dejected. Us both going our separate ways as losers. Kind of a sad-trumpets ending to this story.

Not that this has the makings of a true romance. Not even close.

Is this even romance? Maybe it's just pure lust.

I wonder if I should text him and propose that the person who gets the most wins.

At least one of us will be a winner then. Me, hopefully. I know I can get nine out of ten.

Yes. That's what I'll do.

Me: ***What if the winner is the person who gets the most before we board?***

Him: ***Nope. All or nothing.***

You scared?

Me: ***No. Do you really think you're going to find all of yours?***

Him: ***Damn straight.***

Ugh. What a cocky bastard.

I step out of the gift shop, take the roll of Life Savers out of my bag, peel it open, and start to suck on one, as Robin jogs up to me. "Yep. They're triplets."

I offer her the roll, and she takes one, popping it into her mouth. "Cool."

"How'd you do?"

I give her a big thumbs down.

Robin sighs and starts to tap her tongue ring against the Life Saver, thinking.

I start to walk over to the triplets so I can take their picture when my phone buzzes. The text from Noah says, ***Cute. Mary Anne Evans = George Eliot.***

The picture is a photograph from the back cover of a book that must've been in one of the bookstores, *Silas Marner.*

Darn. Didn't think he'd get that one.

Me: ***You're smart.***

Him: ***You overestimate my literary prowess. I just had a nice bookseller take pity on me.***

Me: ***Aw. Give up?***

Him: ***Never. I'm in it to win it.***

Me: ***You won't.***

Him: ***We each have five.***

I go over to the triplets, snap their picture, and send it to him.

Me: ***Nope. I'm ahead.***

A second later, he texts me a picture of a blond man with a horrendous sunburn.

Then he sends me a picture of a woman holding a paisley bag.

Then a little boy, wearing a neck pillow that looks like a cow.

Holy fuck.

Him: ***Surrender. I'll make it worth your while***

Me: ***I'll make it worth your while when you find #10***

Him: ***Believe me, it'll be worth your while when YOU find #10***

Right. I'm sure a shark's tooth will change my life. The only way it'll be worth my while is when I win and get my movie premiere wish granted. The end. I'm tired, and still buzzed, and I think even those once-uncomfy-looking airport chairs are starting to look good. I stifle a yawn and replace it with my game face.

Me: ***I'm not giving up.***

Him: ***Neither am I.***

Robin grabs my arm, nearly pulling it from its socket as she turns me in the direction of a tall, lanky man in jeans and a cowboy hat. I snap the picture and text it to him.

Him: ***I just need three more. As do you.***

Found that shark's tooth yet?

Grrr. Okay. There's got to be a shark's tooth somewhere around here. I'm just not thinking of it right. I start scanning the walls around me, the people, as if it'll just jump out at me if I look hard enough.

Me: ***I will. Count on it.***

Him: ***If you say so. And Rebecca?***

Me: ***Yes?***

Him: ***Have you ever fucked in the back seat of a cab? Because I don't think I can wait until we get to the hotel.***

chapter eight

Noah

I'm so close I can almost feel her, writhing under me.

The man in the seat next to me is a professional basketball player. Or was. His name is Eduardo, and once upon a time, many years ago, he played for the Boston Celtics. He's about seven feet tall and has hands twice the size of mine.

I don't watch sports, but when I saw *that*, I had the distinct feeling that the man was an athlete. So I sat across from him and struck up a conversation.

Pretended I was a fan.

Asked for a selfie, which he only agreed to when I told him who I was and showed him pictures of me on the set. Turns out, he's a big fan of those Galaxy Titans movies.

Him and about eighty million other people.

"So you're really Megalith?" he says, looking me over from head to toe.

"Yep. I'm a little…larger on screen. Make-up and movie magic."

He squints, and there's a nod of recognition there. "Yeah. I see it now."

Him and nobody else.

When I finish snapping the picture, he shakes my hand, draws me into a one-armed hug. "Hey. Noah Steele. Really cool meeting you. Can't wait to see you in your next flick. Hope you finally put an end to that BuzzKill fuck."

I look around, glad there's no one else to hear him and blow my cover. Not that anyone would believe it, anyway. "Cool to meet you, too, man. Take care. Safe flight."

The second he stands to his enormous height and starts to walk away, I text the picture to Rebecca.

Her: ***Who the fuck is that?***

Me: ***Google him. Eduardo Something. He's a former Boston Celtic.***

Her: ***Never heard of him.***

Me: ***You didn't say how famous. You just said famous.***

Her: ***Hmmm. I guess I'll let it count. Find my laptop yet?***

Me: ***I will. Find my shark's tooth?***

She doesn't respond. I know she's been squirming. I've been sending her dirty messages telling her what I'm going to do to her when I finally win.

Her: ***I'm still winning.***

I scan the list. Had I forgotten something? Oh. Right. The Texas driver's license.

I don't think I can count on her to help me win by forking over hers.

Not a problem.

Once I send the picture of the license to her, we'll be neck and neck, each with just one thing left to find.

One impossible thing.

Though she could easily find that last thing on her list, if she looked hard enough.

I'm not giving her any help.

On the other hand, it's more than likely the Mac has left the building. Why would someone steal the damn thing and then just hang around, waiting to be caught?

Still. Holding onto hope. Digging deep.

Whatever buzz I had before is almost gone, now. We've been at this game for three hours. Three hours we could've been together, tasting, teasing, fucking each other. Yeah, it's a waste, but so would be leaving this airport without even trying. I want her that bad.

I've been dying for a coffee and I'm pretty much dead on my feet. It's just after four and the airport is starting to come alive with people getting to their gates for early morning flights.

Dammit. I liked it when it was quiet. More intimate.

Me: ***Not for long.***

I like playing with her. Even if I know I can't win this. I can tell throwing around the ego riles her up. And I love to get her riled.

Even if there's no way I can win this.

But at least I can tie things up.

I reach into the back pocket of my jeans to get my wallet and even the score.

Then I reach for my other pocket. I rip up my jacket and search those pockets. My carry-on. Every pocket I can think of. I find my passport, earphones, a pack of chewing gum, my clear plastic bag with my under-3.4 oz liquids.

But fuck me hard.

My wallet is gone.

chapter nine

Becka

At six in the morning, I say goodbye to Robin, whose flight is leaving at six-thirty, at her gate. She hugs me and says, "Good luck, girl! Text me who wins!"

I wave to her. "I will. Thanks for everything. Have a good flight."

Then I go to the restrooms to wash up. I splash cold water on my face, brush my teeth, spritz some perfume, reapply my lip gloss and brush my hair.

Better. But not good.

Not as good as *some* people. Like a particular movie star I know.

God, twenty-four hours awake has done me no favors. I look like the living dead. I yawn, just staring at my raccoon-eyed, sallow-skinned, droopy face in the mirror.

How does Noah Steele even like me? I'm not butt-ugly, but I'm definitely…vanilla. Isn't Hollywood full of pretty faces? How do I even compare? Especially looking like this.

It's chillier now, so I reach into my carry-on and pull on my cashmere cardigan. Then I go to a little juice bar and buy myself a muffin and a coffee. I have a beast of a hangover, which I always get from mixing hard liquor and beer.

I sit there, picking at the muffin and wishing I had a blanket and pillow to curl up with. Even my favorite, fluffy cardigan isn't cutting it. My body tingles with exhaustion, reaching deep into my bones. My eyes keep trying to drag themselves closed.

I open them when someone slumps into the chair beside me.

Noah.

He throws his leather jacket atop his carry-on on the chair beside him and scrubs a hand over his face. "Shit, I'm tired."

I hold up my coffee. "Extra-huge. For that reason."

He eyes it with longing. "Looks good."

I reach into my pocket and pull out a crumpled five. "Let me buy you one. It's the least I can do after you footed the bill for mine last night."

He palms the money with no argument, stands, and suddenly vises my head between his hands. He kisses me on the forehead. "Bless you."

I can only stare after him, wondering what the hell has gotten into him. As he lumbers away, he looks like an old man, like he's suffering worse than I am.

Gone is that cocky bastard I once knew. Maybe his ego is asleep.

When he returns with his coffee, I say, "Are you okay?"

He takes the lid off the cup and swallows a gulp. "I will be."

He settles down next to me and starts to stare at my thighs. Or, not at my thighs. At the muffin on my thighs. “Um. Do you want some?”

“Don’t you…”

I shake my head. “Not that hungry.”

He breaks a piece off and scoops it into his mouth.

“Better?” I ask him.

He nods and looks over at me with a defeated look. “Lost my wallet.”

My jaw drops. “What?”

He shrugs. “Looked all over for it.”

I sit back, stunned. “Gosh. Well. When was the last time you had it?”

“With you. At dinner. Or…just after that. I tried to retrace my steps but I’ve been all over this terminal and I have no clue where it could be now.”

“Did you go to the TSA?”

He nods, working his jaw. “That’s where I just came from.”

“Oh, my gosh. I’m so sorry.” I suck in a breath, and then let it out. “It’s almost unbelievable. Don’t you think it’s a weird coincidence? Us both losing things like that?”

“What? You think it’s a conspiracy?”

I shrug. “Could be.”

“You are entirely too suspicious, you know that?” He manages to draw one corner of his mouth up in a smile that twists my insides. “All I know is I was running all over this damn place trying to snap pictures of the things on your list. It must’ve just come out of my pocket somewhere.”

Fine. I’m too suspicious. He’s probably right. That’s my writer’s mind creating drama where there is none.

His mouth twists. "So tell me. What would Ben do in this situation?"

Ben? Who is…oh, right. "Well, he'd—"

"I'll tell you. He's a billionaire. He wouldn't give a shit. Also, he's perfect, so this kind of shit wouldn't happen to him in the first place, because he probably has people who handle the people who handle the people who handle his wallet."

I'm shaking my head. "No…" I start. "He has flaws."

"Let me guess. He's broken from a child tragedy that has pushed him to succeed. He has trouble opening up and loving Leia because of it."

I frown at him.

I frigging hate him.

He shakes his head. "Jesus. I'm right again?"

I don't get his tone. Like he's disappointed in me. What the fuck did I do to him?

"Hey. Just because you lost your wallet is no reason to take it out on me. I might not be the greatest writer on earth but you don't have to make fun of my ideas."

"I'm not. I'm just saying that maybe if you had an original idea, you'd get somewhere."

I open my mouth. He did not just say that. "What?"

He rips his baseball cap out of his bag, fixes it down low over his eyes, sinks into his chair, and crosses his arms. "You heard me."

I pull myself to the edge of the seat and put my hands on my hips. "Look, Mr. Expert on Everything. I write the stories and characters that speak to me. To me. If people don't like it, they don't have to read it. It has nothing to do with you."

He lifts the brim of his baseball hat. "Like hell it doesn't. If you weren't so goddamn wrapped up in perfect Ben, we'd be waking up this morning after the best night of sex of our lives and feeding each other waffles. I'd be licking syrup off those perfect breasts of yours. It'd be fan-fucking-tastic. Instead, where the fuck are we right now? In hell?"

I stare at him, and the only thing that comes to mind right then is… I like waffles.

Also, the image he puts in my mind is delicious enough to bring tears to my eyes. Poof. Gone.

I am such an asshole.

"Fuck. Me." He scrubs his hands over his face. "Yeah. You know. I'm sorry. You're right. It has nothing to do with me."

"No. You're right." I collapse in the seat and sink down, miserably. It's an a-ha moment. All the stories on that laptop are just like he said. Cliché. Boring. My made-up idea of the perfect romance.

A big, ball-of-suck, a-ha moment.

Now he's looking out the window, toward a plane that is just landing, taxiing into the runway, or maybe beyond that, where I can just make out the tops of the skyscrapers of the city. "You ever feel like a city hates you?"

I stare at him. I remember thinking that, just yesterday.

"Yeah. First I lose my dignity, then I lose my wallet. Now I'm going to lose the girl."

"Me?" I straighten, lean forward, brush his arm with my fingertips. "I'm right here."

"But." He holds up a finger between us. "We have under five hours until we leave, Texas. And I might be an asshole, but I'm not so much of an asshole that even if I magically produced your laptop, or you somehow took pity on me and said yes right now, I'd make *you* pay for the hotel."

I rub the arms of my fuzzy cardigan, speechless.

And right then, I know it like I know my own name.

I made the wrong decision, turning him down.

Who the fuck cared if this was just one night?

I want Noah. With every little pore in my body.

And now it's too late. It's morning.

He says, "I shouldn't have said what I said. I was frustrated. I know nothing about romance novels, really. I'm sure your stories are amazing."

No. He knows everything. He's right.

I open my mouth, ready to confess, to tell him he's been right about everything, and I made a mistake. To tell him that he pushes all my buttons to on like no one ever has and I want it as much as he wants it. "Listen…"

But he's already looking away from me, standing up. "Guess I'd better figure out a way to get my credit cards canceled. Hey. Watch my stuff, will you?"

I watch helplessly as he walks away, sipping on his coffee, and starts to speak to someone at a nearby podium. I watch him gesturing the way I had with my laptop.

I frown.

This would make the worst fucking romance novel in the world.

But I don't care.

I open up a text to him. ***Meet me in the family restroom in 5?***

I watch him across the airport. He must have the phone on vibrate because he stops suddenly, reaches into his pocket, and fishes it out.

Then he whirls and looks at me, his eyes wide, all sense of control gone.

And I know I won't regret it for a second. It's so worth it, if only for that exquisitely stunned look that completely lights his face.

chapter ten

Noah

I'm just finishing up a conversation with an especially unhelpful airport employee with a Brooklynn accent when I get the text.

I read it.

And suddenly, nothing matters. Not the disastrous audition, or the scavenger hunt, or my missing wallet.

Fuck it all.

I look up at her, at those big green eyes, fastened on me.

She smiles.

Hell yes. That's not exactly what I text her back. It's more like: ***Hell. Fucking. Yes.*** With my fingers shaking on the keyboard like I'm some teenage virgin.

She stands, smooths her skirt down, and lifts her bag. She points to my stuff, to remind me it's still there, and to not lose my head and run off without it. Good point. I can't afford to lose anything else during this trip.

Then she fluffs her messy bun and heads off, away from me, toward the nearest set of restrooms.

Holy. Fucking. Shit.

I look back at my phone, to make sure I didn't hallucinate the message due to lack of sleep.

Nope. Still there.

I head over to my stuff, every nerve in my body doing a victory dance. I grab my carry-on and head to the opposite men's room. I take off my hat, push my hair back, make sure I don't smell like shit, considering I haven't showered in over thirty-six hours. Pulling back the zipper on my bag, I grab my toothbrush, brushing my teeth for the second time this morning. I wash my face and change into a different t-shirt.

I should have more control over myself.

I feel like a kid on prom night.

It might be the sleep deprivation.

But suddenly, this city is the best fucking city in the world.

Packing my stuff, I throw my carry-on over my shoulder, hook my jacket over it, and head out of the restroom with all the energy of a sugared-up kid.

I practically skip to the family restroom, my pulse throbbing in my neck as I stop in front of the door to the family restroom.

I grit my teeth, count to ten to calm my breathing. I knock on the door.

Wait. Look around.

No answer.

Then I knock again. Louder.

Wait more. No answer.

And I'm right where I was back before I got Rebecca's text.

Hating this goddamn city.

chapter eleven

Becka

I press myself against the giant, three-sided advertising pillar in the center of the concourse, with a light-up ad for mobile phone service.

I wish it would swallow me up.

I read this morning's text conversation with Lily again, trying to figure out where everything went so wrong. Last night, I'd texted her, so happy that I'd met Brock. THE Brock. That was all.

That was such a lighthearted, happy time.

Now?

Lily: ***OMG SERIOUSLY?***

Sorry, just turned on my phone after all-night studying

Me: ***You will not believe what's happened since then. We all-night flirted. He's even more beautiful in person. And sweet. And funny…***

Lily: ***And???***

Me: ***I'm seriously into him. I think we're going to do it. Right now. I'm standing here in the family restroom, waiting for him.***

Lily: ***!!! Go girl!!!***

Me: ***I can't believe it! Me and Brock???!!!***

Lily: ***You and Brock??? Fuck that. You and MEGALITH!!***

Me: ***Wait… Who?***

She then proceeded to send me a shitload of articles. Articles about Noah Steele. His IMDB profile. A piece about him purchasing a house in Hollywood Hills for $6.5 million. Pictures of Noah sitting comfortably next to Hollywood A-listers like Scarlett Johansson, Jennifer Lawrence, and Gal Gadot at a panel at Comic-Con.

What the actual fuck?

So it turns out…my Noah, the sweet, nice but desperately gorgeous up-and-coming film actor is not really up-and-coming.

He's already come. Bigtime. All over my face.

Because he's only a superhero…he's also part of one of the most successful film franchises of all time.

Something called Galaxy Titans.

Apparently, he's Megalith, this giant blue rock dude who parades around in nothing but a loincloth, can crush mountains with his mind, and has abs you can grate cheese on.

This small detail must have conveniently slipped his mind when he was talking to me.

After reading those articles, my stomach sinking down to my toes, I'd run from the bathroom, the overwhelming desire in my abdomen giving way to overwhelming mortification.

I felt like I was going to throw up.

It's one thing to have a one-night stand with a man I'll never see again.

But he's a bona-fide, A-list, dyed-in-the-wool *movie star.*

I try to catch my breath. The airport spins around me. My heart is beating so hard it hurts.

Me: ***OMGOMGOMGOMG***

Lily: ***Are you okay?***

Me: ***Noooooooooo! I didn't know! I can't do this! Not with him!***

Lily: ***Why???????***

Me: ***Because he's a movie star!***

Lily: ***So? You were okay when it was Brock, but you're not okay now that he's Megalith? You're crazy.***

Me: ***In that one picture he looks awfully chummy with Gal Gadot. What the fuck does he want with me??***

Lily: ***Go to the family restroom and find out!!***

Me: ***FML***

Lily: ***BECKA. I COMMAND YOU TO GO. NOW. THE FATE OF THE GALAXY IS IN YOUR HANDS.***

(And text me back. I'll answer as soon as I can. Getting ready for the bar exam right now.)

This is the part where I'd text her back a good luck. But I can't. I'm too mortified.

Leaning to my right, I peek around the pillar, toward the block of restrooms, like someone who's being chased by an ax-murderer.

I catch him—Noah Steele, the A-list movie star—standing there, outside the restroom, a confused expression on his face as he scans the airport.

Oh, of course he's a movie star. He's too lethally beautiful to be an actual human, like me.

I'm sighing at his beauty, at all those chiseled features that are too perfect and masculine to be real, as his stony gray eyes drift my way.

Letting out a squeak deep in my throat, I whip my head back, pressing myself hard against the other side of the pillar. I hope to all fuck he didn't see me.

Because not only would it make it more obvious how far out of his league I am, it'd also make me look like a fucking lunatic.

As I'm standing there, stiff, shaking, thinking another panic attack is a definite possibility, an older man in a three-piece suit approaches me. "Are you all right, miss?" he asks me.

It's then I notice that there are about ten other people watching me from this side of the pillar, probably thinking I've lost my shit.

I haven't been in New York long, but one thing I've learned is that people here have seen a lot of nutty shit. I was only here a couple weeks, barely got out, but still caught a fully naked guy playing a sax in Times Square, Elmo humping a woman on the street, and a guy walking a pet cheetah. Nobody around me even batted an eyelash. In order to get people worried, you have to be looking a lot crazier than your normal, everyday crazy.

I guess I qualify.

"Oh. Er…yes. Fine, thanks."

I even manage a feeble smile.

He nods and heads off toward his gate, leaving me alone. I pretend to be reading something interesting on my phone, and one-by-one, the rest of my audience loses interest.

Once they do, I crane my neck to my right, ever-so-slowly, around the pillar to see if he's still there.

But he's not.

Of course he's not.

He's a big movie star, with big things to do.

I, on the other hand, am just a small thing. A blip.

Straightening, I let out a relieved sigh and check my phone. Only four hours and I can haul my ass home and get some sleep and forget this ever happened.

That's when I feel a presence hovering at my left that wasn't there before.

I slowly turn my head.

He's leaning with his forearm up against the pillar, looking down at me.

"Did you get lost?" he says, with a world-ending smile.

chapter twelve

Noah

This woman is going to be the death of me.

My cock is so damn hard for her now, and she hasn't even touched me. Her face turns pinker as she looks up at me, and it's all I can do not to pull her against my body.

"That was some joke you played," I say, my voice low and controlled. "Are you happy with yourself?"

She looks away, out the windows, toward the runway.

"I might have confused you, with the scavenger hunt," I say to her, leaning in closer. "But I don't play games with little girls."

Her eyes snap to mine. "You don't play games? Then what's this?"

She holds her phone in front of me, but she's suddenly shaking so hard I can't read it. I grab her wrist to steady it and the first thing I see is the CGI-enhanced, bulging body of Megalith, filling her screen.

Fuck. That asshole, again.

I straighten, my fingers digging into her wrist. "What? It's me. So what?"

"So what?" she repeats, louder now. "You didn't tell me you were this big-deal movie star!"

I look around. Nobody seems to overhear. I shrug. "What does that matter?"

"Because!" she blurts, tearing her wrist from me and holding her hands up. "It just does!"

"And…why? Give me a good reason why it matters."

She presses her lips together. "It doesn't matter that you are. It matters that you felt you needed to keep it from me."

I dig my hands into my pockets and hitch a shoulder. "I didn't keep it from you. I just didn't tell you. People act differently toward me when they know."

She throws up her hands. "I wouldn't have! I don't care what you do!"

"Yeah, you do. You're acting that way now," I point out, dragging a hand down my face.

"Because you lied to me! Here I thought you and I had so much in common with our careers. But you're…" She closes her eyes and lets out a long sigh. "This successful big shot who probably spends all his flights coaxing women into hotel rooms with him."

So that was it. I stalk away from her, then come up close, to her face. "I don't *coax women anywhere.*" I repeat her words. "That's not who I am."

"But you can't deny you're successful."

I let out a laugh. "Are you fucking kidding me? So you want me to be a loser? Is that right?"

She nods. "Yeah. I guess. I want you to be a loser, like me."

"You're not a loser. Fuck, why would you even say that?" I try to grab for her hand but she flinches away.

"I felt like we connected. But now, I don't know. You're...people like you don't fall for people like me. It just doesn't happen."

I stare at her, but she says it matter-of-factly, like she doesn't have any idea how gorgeous she is and under-my-skin she's become.

"What? Are you serious? What is a person *like you?* Tell me."

"Someone who's been pretending in her career for all her life and who's slept with all of two guys…count them…one—two—" She's counting off on her fingers, her cheeks as red as two cherries. "In her entire pathetic life! And they were both total assholes!"

"You've got to be kidding. I look at you and I think you're so fucking amazing. You have your art and you pursue it and you don't fucking let anyone tell you how to change it. You're going to write this book and it's going to be incredible. Because you don't give up, and you refuse to change to please anyone else."

She gives me a doubtful look. "Stop. You haven't even read it."

"I don't have to. I see a passion inside you. You love what you do. It's in your eyes. I used to have that, too."

She blinks, surprised. "Used to?"

"Megalith is a fucking prison for me. Do you understand? I didn't tell you about him because I fucking hate him. I used to be a real actor."

She opens her mouth, but closes it, suddenly speechless. I can tell that whatever she was going to say, she's rethinking it.

"But you are," she protests, her voice softer now. "I saw *Going Home.* Thousands of people saw it. You were almost nominated for an Oscar. You're the real thing."

"Maybe I was, once. Not anymore. I used to get those meaty roles. But I sold out to play that asshole of a superhero and now I can't get a serious role to save my life. All producers want me to do is show my dimples and my abs. They tell me I lack the emotional depth to play the lead role. So excuse me if I tell Megalith to go fuck himself every once in a while and just try to stand on my own.

"Also, I'll have you know that there are about twelve direct flights that I could've taken between yesterday evening and eleven-twenty-five this morning that would've gotten me into LAX a hell of a lot sooner. But I booked myself on *your* flight for a reason. Because I wanted to get to know you. I had a feeling that even if I had a worthless audition, *you* could make this fucked-up trip from hell worth my while."

"I…" Are those tears in her eyes? "I don't know what to say."

I shrug. "You already said it. When you recognized me as Brock. When you told me you loved what I'd done. When you quoted me back to me? God…that was fucking incredible. You don't know how much I needed to hear that, after the day I'd had."

She looks up to me, and the guilt on her face nearly tears my heart to pieces.

"So thank you for that. But I get it. I'll leave you alone."

I take a step back.

But before I can turn and leave, she reaches for me, fisting my t-shirt in her hand and pressing her mouth onto mine.

chapter thirteen

Becka

Once again, I don't know how it happens. It must be a super-hero trick.

One moment, I'm furious at him. I'll be happy if I never see him again. Noah. Brock. Megalith. All of them.

The next moment, I've pulled him down to my level, kissing him for all I'm worth, my hands grabbing huge fistfuls of his shirt, feeling the rock-solid muscles underneath.

Not just kissing. Assaulting him with my tongue.

He isn't expecting it, but a second later he starts to respond. Taking control. And everything else fades away. He kisses me and my body tingles, coming alive.

When he breaks the kiss he says my name, breathless, *Rebecca,* just like that, like a song, so full of raw need.

Better than Ben the Fucking Lame Billionaire ever could.

He reaches a finger up and strokes the side of my face. His smile is half-astonishment, half-lust, as his eyes trail over each of my features.

Then his hand slides through my hair, to the nape of my neck and he pulls me toward him, capturing my mouth in another kiss.

The tingling throughout my body intensifies. My knees weaken. I hate PDAs but all the other people around us are gone now. So is Megalith, and Ben and Leia, and all the other assholes. All I think, see and feel is him.

After a moment of nibbling on his lips, he pulls away slowly. “What do you want?” he asks me.

I only have to glance toward the family restroom to make my thoughts known.

He takes my hand and guides me there. Thank god it is unoccupied. I don’t think I could live if I have to wait one more minute. He pulls the door open, and we slide inside, throwing our bags unceremoniously onto the floor.

He pushes me against the wall. I gasp as immediately his lips are back on mine. This time all gentleness has gone and in its place is raw passion.

My arms move around him and my hands clasp around his neck. His hands grip my waist and pull me close. I shudder as I feel our bodies touch. Even through clothes, it’s just too good.

His kiss deepens and I feel his tongue pushing its way between my lips. As our tongues dance together his hands move down to my ass and pull me closer still. Already I can feel his erection through his jeans, and I move my hips gently, rubbing against him. He groans into my mouth and I feel his fingers seeking out the hem of my skirt, seeking out what’s underneath.

We pull away for a moment, gasping for breath, eyes locked.

His hands slide upwards, sliding up the globes of my ass. The touch of his big, warm hands on my bare skin makes me shudder. Our lips join again, and his hands move around to my front, under my shirt to my stomach. As they move upwards I hold my breath and wait, desperate for him to touch me more, to be closer to him. His fingers trail up my sides, brushing along the edges of my breasts, making me gasp a little. They trail across the top of my breasts, gently teasing my skin. A finger slides under the edge of my bra, flirting with the fabric, touching me, but not touching me. He traces a finger down my cleavage, moving back up and away again. Driving me crazy. Making me desperate.

"Oh, god, please," I murmur, pulling my mouth away from his kiss. "Don't tease me."

"Who's teasing?" He grins at me and bends to bite my bottom lip, tugging it gently with his teeth.

"Bastard," I mutter. "You're punishing me, aren't you? For not meeting you a few minutes ago?"

"No," he says. "I'm punishing you because this could've been in a nice, five-star hotel. My treat."

Without warning, he grasps the bottom hem of my shirt and yanks it up and over my head. He stops, leaving all the fabric twisted around my arms, holding them high above my head so I'm stretched there.

I shiver slightly as the cool air hits my skin, chest heaving.

His gaze moves hungrily over my body, his breath warm on my skin. His eyes greedily take in my breasts, encased in a black silk bra.

Still holding my hands up over my head, he licks my earlobe. His mouth, hot and open, trails down the side of my neck. I tilt my head to the ceiling and my eyes roll back, sparks igniting everywhere in my vision.

Fuck. I don't need the hotel. I just need his talented tongue.

I let out another gasp as his tongue slides down my collarbone, licking its way around my nipple through the lace covering. He takes it between his teeth and tugs on it slightly, flicking it with his tongue.

HOLY.

That is the only word I know right now. It's a holy experience. I arch my back off the cold tile wall, offering my breast to him for more.

His hand encircles both of mine above me, pinning me there as he sweeps his other hand down my bare arm. With his finger, he tugs the right cup down, freeing the nipple. He encircles my tit with his hand, molding it, then sucks it into his mouth.

My pussy clenches. The heat is almost too much, from my breasts down deep within my core. "Now," I tell him. "Just fuck me. Fuck me now."

I shouldn't have said it, because now I think he's going to torture me more. His movements become even more slow and languid, like we have all the time in the world. His teeth clamp around the lace of the left cup and he drags that down, too.

"Perfect tits."

He ducks his head down and sucks on the left one. Bites it. Flicks it with his tongue. Wets it with his mouth and then blows on it softly.

It's clear he thinks they're something special, with all the attention he's lavishing on them.

And my whole body's loving it. Because I'm going to come.

He hasn't even done anything but kiss my breasts, and I'm already getting close. "All right," I moan, trying to free my wrists from the shackle of his hand. "Just…"

"Not yet." His voice is low. Reprimanding me.

He kisses his way up my neck and to my ear, tugging on the lobe gently while his free hand glides down my side, sliding up under my skirt, delivering feather-light touches to my thigh.

His breath is warm on my ear. "What do you want?"

His fingers dip between my legs, stroking lightly over the sensitive skin. "I already told you."

"Not yet," he says again. "This took work. I'm going to enjoy you. And you're going to let me."

Damn him. He's going to make me beg for it.

He lifts his fingers between my thighs and they slide over the silken fabric of my panties. His finger moves in soft, lazy circles over my mound. I spread my legs, letting him know I'm totally open for business.

As if it isn't completely obvious from how wet I am.

But his finger simply continues to move in those tortuous circles, teasing me through the fabric of my panties. He narrows in on my slit, rubbing along it, and I quake and squirm against him, wanting it faster. Harder. More.

He knows what I want.

Of course he knows.

This is our one, our only time. And he's not just going to make it unforgettable.

He's on track to make it fucking *epic.*

He fastens his mouth on mine hard, thrusting his tongue in and out, fucking my mouth in the way I wish he'd fuck my body. I return the kiss feverishly and struggle to free my arms so I can take control and play with his cock, but he refuses to let go.

I let out a frustrated growl as he presses me so hard against the wall.

"Fuck. Me," I demand as his fingers finally slide under the band of my panties. He teases the lips of my pussy, just dancing over the fine hair there, and it takes all my strength not to cry out. "Please. Noah."

"In time," he says, his voice a low growl.

Am I affecting him *at all?* I know he's a good actor, a great one, but come on. He's completely unruffled, completely unaffected.

It'd help if I could get my hands free and tease him the way he's teasing me.

But dammit, he's so strong.

Then he slides his finger between my lips, gently making contact with my clit.

And I can't even remember why I was so frustrated. My body shudders and I moan. He resumes those steady, soft circles on my clit, then shoves his knee between my legs, thrusting them further apart.

Then, keeping constant pressure of one knuckle on my clit, he inserts a curled finger into my pussy. I cry out.

"That good?" he breathes into my ear. But he knows it is. "If this were the hotel I'd sit your sweet little Texas ass on my face and fuck you with my tongue. But you're just going to have to settle for this."

It's not settling. Oh, fuck, it's not even close. I don't think I've ever felt better. His finger slides out, pushing back in, setting up a rhythm, all the while keeping steady pressure with his knuckle on my clit. In. Out. In.

When he adds another one, my pussy walls clenching around him, I realize I'm moaning, non-stop. Rocking on his hand and moaning so loud, people outside have to hear.

He doesn't tell me to be quiet. From the superior look on his face, I think he wants people to know what he's doing to me in here. That he owns me. Is that my punishment for not meeting him initially? Or is it my reward for being here—right now—so very ready to—

I scream, louder than I ever have, pushing down onto his hand as the orgasm rips through me. I lose control as his fingers move in a tornado of heat inside me.

Noah lets go of my wrists and wraps that hand around my waist, holding me up as I come, and come, and come, my body wracked with convulsions. He kisses me hard on the mouth as the shuddering subsides, his fingers still inside me, still stroking my clit.

Finally able to move, I take my shirt off, toss it onto my bag, and remove my bra completely. He ducks his head and licks at my breasts again.

"Quit teasing, Brock. Do me now," I part growl, part moan at him, gripping his cock through his jeans. It's already rock hard. "Please."

This time, he watches me in awe as he lets me access to the buttons on his jeans. I quickly tear at them, snapping the button, ripping the fly. I take his cock in my hand. God, it's hot, and as I free it from his jeans, I realize it's…huge.

They say everything's bigger in Texas, but I swear I've never seen a cock this huge. I stroke its length, from the mushroom head to the base. Holy shit. I feel myself get wet again, licking my lips as I meet his intense ashy-gray eyes. "I need this inside me now."

"Don't think I don't want this as much as you do," he grinds out, and I see the break of lust in his eyes. Like maybe, just maybe, this is affecting him, too. "But, damn, Rebecca... here?"

I run my fingers over his amazing

perfect

gorgeous

dick.

"It's all we'll ever get."

Noah clenches his jaw and positions himself between my legs, and cradling my ass, hooks my leg around his hips, so I can feel the tip of his cock bumping against my panties. A tremor shakes through me. I shove his jeans down to his thighs and he grips himself in his hand, nudging aside my panties and sliding himself up and against my slit.

Oh god, please.

I'm so wet, and Noah's doing it again, teasing me, running the tip of his cock up and down my sex. And just when he starts to grip my hips and drive it home, he pauses.

"Fuck," he says suddenly.

"What?"

"I had a condom. *In my wallet.*"

Shit. "Are you clean? I'm on the pill."

He nods, and sensing what I'll say, slides the tip of his cock to my opening. My lips part, like my whole body is opening for him. He curses under his breath and dives downward to crush my mouth beneath his, and while he tongues me, he drives in with one hard, quick thrust that pushes the full, huge length into me.

My back arches against the cold tile, and I let out a rapturous cry.

He holds still inside me for a second. Nothing moving but our hearts beating like crazy against each other's skin. His breath hot on mine. His mouth and mine start moving, tasting, kissing. My pussy walls grip him tightly. He kisses my mouth more deeply, grabbing onto my legs, pushing the full power of his body impossibly close to me, burying himself fully inside. He slides his cock out, pausing when just the tip is still inside. Then he pushes back in, forcing all the air out of my lungs. God, it's even deeper this time.

His hands tighten on my hips. His shoes scrabble on the slick tile floor for purchase as I drop my gaze to peer between us, at his hard cock sliding into me. It turns me on more, watching his body working, watching him finally starting to come undone.

I start pushing my hips down to meet his thrusts. He quickens his pace and starts to slam against my body, gripping my hips and pulling me down onto him. My head falls back against the wall. I reach my hands under his t-shirt scrape my fingernails up his sculpted back.

The pressure of his pelvis grinding on my clit is too much, and suddenly I'm on the brink of oblivion again. He's thrusting as I shudder. His grip on my hips tightens and he pushes in, as hard as he can. Heat and liquid fills me as he lets out an animal groan, tensing against me. I grip him inside me, wrapping my arms and legs tightly around him, holding his rock-hard body there as he comes.

When I'm still impaled on his cock, sweaty, flushed…it starts to hit me. I'm half naked in the airport restroom. Impaled on Brock's… Megalith's… Noah Steele's super cock.

But I'm happy.

God, so happy.

"So it's true," I say to him as he slumps against me and rests his forehead on mine. "Megalith can level mountains."

He doesn't say a word. He lifts me off him and settles me on the ground. He hands me a wad of paper towels to clean myself up.

"Aren't you going to say anything?" I ask him as I wipe the stiff paper between my legs, feeling the beginnings of guilt creeping in. I get defensive. "Or are you going to be an asshole about it?"

Before it can settle, he moves swiftly against me, pressing his hard body against mine and kissing me silly. Kissing me in answer. A kiss that feels…happy.

And I don't know. This gross bathroom with its cracked tile, horrible lighting, full garbage can, and rancid smell?

It's actually kind of romantic, to me.

chapter fourteen

Noah

I'm sitting on at the Gate 14, the gate for the flight to Dallas-Fort Worth, with Rebecca's head pressed up against my arm, a shit-eating grin on my face. We're both using the same outlet to charge our phones.

She's sleeping, her eyelids fluttering. I won't move too much and wake her, because I'd like to think that flutter means her bitch muse has finally gotten her act together and is doing her thing.

"You make a sweet couple," a hunched old lady with a cane says to me as she passes by, the *New York Times* stuffed under her arm.

I nod in return, not so much annoyed by the intrusion as I am by the knowledge that in another two hours, this "couple" will become unlinked.

She lets out a small noise and her eyes flicker open, pupils landing on me before her eyes drift slowly closed again.

Her voice is sing-songy with drowsiness. "Don't you want to sleep?"

And miss this moment, this first time in weeks where I finally feel satisfied with myself? Hell, no. I shake my head.

She yawns. "Hey. What seat do you have on the flight?"

"Uh." I check my phone. "12B."

"Ugh. Really? I'm 34E."

I wince. "That's probably the worst seat on the whole plane."

Her eyes blink fully open now. I've worried her. "Really? Why? I'm more likely to die if the plane goes down?"

"No. If the plane goes down, we're probably all dead." I count off on my hand. "One. Middle seat. Two. Back of the plane. Three. Not anywhere near me. That's the big one."

"Oh. Maybe the flight won't be full? Or someone will trade with one of us?"

"Not likely."

She stretches her spine, wiping her eyes. "What are you thinking?" She looks closely at me, tapping my forehead. "Wait. I can read your mind. Really? So…you want to trade with me? How nice of you! I accept."

I shake my head slowly. "That won't solve number three. And stop. You couldn't pay me to trade with you."

"Okay. I can't pay you, but maybe…" She winks.

"Now you're tapping in to what I'm thinking," I say, scanning the faces of the people around us. "But I also think they're on to us. That family restroom is probably off-limits."

More than a few heads turned when we stepped out of the restroom together, so flushed it was obvious what we were up to. A lot of whispering and nudging ensued, and we're still fielding curious looks from people. It's like they expect us to get busy right in front of them.

My arm is draped around her, and she's contemplating and slowly stroking the hairs on my forearm. "I'm sure there are other restrooms. Or…what about the mile-high club?"

"Joining the mile-high club is nearly impossible. I don't think it's as fun as it sounds. I can barely fit my own ass in those restrooms."

"True," she sighs, nodding slowly.

"That doesn't mean I'm unwilling to try, though."

She lets out a laugh. "That makes two of us."

I duck my head to kiss her, long and slow, and stroke my hand up her thigh. "Mmm. I don't know if I can wait until then."

"Oh yeah?"

"Really. What can I say? You inspire me."

"Wow. Inspiring Megalith. That's like moving mountains."

I frown at her, only partially kidding. Nothing can sour the taste of her on my tongue, but that comes close. "You had to mention him?"

She pouts. "Sorry. Sorry. You really hate him, don't you?"

I nod and check the time on my phone. "Yeah. You know. It's all CGI, so any idiot could play him."

"I sincerely doubt that."

"You've never seen Galaxy Titans. How do you know?"

"So?" She shrugs. "I think I may have seen bits and pieces of it. Men with tights and capes and hard bodies, running around, flexing their muscles…lots of explosions…right?"

"Yeah. Dead on."

"I'm sure you're great at that. Just like you're sure I write great stories, even though you've never read them."

I let out a sour laugh, take out my phone and find a YouTube video of one of my more emotional scenes, the defining moment in my character arc where my best friend dies in a train wreck and I make up my mind to exact revenge on the villain, BuzzKill.

She sits up, yawns and stretches, watching. When it's over, she says, "Wow." Her eyes drift below, to my t-shirt, and I know she's wondering if those abs in the movie are real. "That's…good. But now I feel bad. You can show me your work, but I can't show you mine. I don't have my laptop."

"But you're going to leave without it? You can write something new?"

She nods. "Yeah. Maybe. I think so. I know neither of us found all the items on the scavenger hunt. But I feel like I won, anyway."

"You won?" I shake my head. "I kicked your ass."

"*Please*." She considers it for a moment. "Tie?"

I concede. We shake hands.

She takes her phone from the charger and frowns at it. "Shoot. My phone isn't charging. I only have six percent. What time is it?"

"Ten." We have just under an hour before the plane begins boarding.

She jiggles the charger, then groans and tucks her phone into her bag. "So, where you live in L.A.…" she ventures. "Do you have celebrity neighbors?"

"As a matter of fact, I share a property border with Sofia Vergara."

She claps her hands excitedly. “That’s so cool. Do you have a pool?”

“I do. Saltwater. On top of a mountain, overlooking the city.”

I pick up my phone and start to scroll through pictures for her.

“See? Now that would be a romantic first date for my book.”

“Not the place. Always the—”

“Person,” she finishes. “Yeah yeah yeah. I know.” The slideshow starts with pictures of my angular, modern home on a mountain, then goes into some appearances from last Comic-Con tour, with Bradley Cooper, Robert Downey Jr, and Chris Pratt. She’s quite the fangirl when it comes to famous people, I’m starting to realize, calling out each name and grabbing the phone out of my hand to ogle them. It makes it even more unbelievable that she doesn’t know who I am.

Of course, those guys all have recent work *other* than superhero movies to their credit.

“I can’t believe,” she gushes, holding the phone so close to her face that her nose nearly bumps the screen, “that you are friends with these guys.”

“Not *friends*. They know my name. That’s about it. I’m minor, compared to them.”

She draws her lower lip into her mouth in that sexy way that damn near kills me. “You look very chummy.”

“We’re actors, remember?” I remind her. “Bullshit is our business. We specialize in making people believe things that aren’t real.”

My phone begins to ring. I check the display. It’s Anne.

I hold up a finger to her and say, "My agent. I have to take this." I answer. "Hey, Anne."

I can tell Anne isn't in a good mood by her tone. Plus, it's seven-thirty there, and she probably hasn't yet had her daily dose of espresso. She says, "All right. Press photos rescheduled. You need to have your ass in the chair tomorrow morning."

I let out a sigh. "Yeah. I'll be there."

"And they reminded me that they're still waiting for your answer on movies seven through nine. Have you signed the contracts yet?"

I have the contracts on the center island of my kitchen. They're in an unopened envelope with the official TriMast Productions—the producers of Galaxy Titans—logo on the return address. Anne spent the past few weeks fine-tuning the language with them, and has gotten me a fantastic deal—five million a picture plus a tiny sliver of the profits. If I'm down, I just need to sign those babies on the dotted line in triplicate and let them fly back home.

I've been putting it off. "Not yet. I'll look them over when I get back home."

She lets out a groan. "Why are you dragging your feet, Steele? You understand it's an eight-figure contract? When will you ever see that kind of money—"

"I understand, but—"

"Look. Noah. I understand what you're trying to do is for your own mental health. You want to prove you have the skills, and you're not just another pretty face. But fuck it, kid. You're talking fifteen mil, even before profits. Pad your wallet first, then worry about being taken seriously."

I press my lips together. Maybe I should. Maybe I'd care more if I was still struggling, money-wise. But goddammit, signing on the dotted line feels like swallowing razor blades. "You get me that audition for next week?"

She makes a clicking sound with her tongue. She's more than disappointed in me. She's offering me filet mignon and I'm asking for a McDonald's burger. I know she cares about me like a mom, but she runs a business, too. Her cut of peanuts compared to her cut of fifteen million will likely be enough for her to disown me.

"Actually, Noah, I wanted to talk to you about that."

That doesn't sound promising. I grip the phone and turn away from Rebecca, who's fiddling with her own phone and the broken charger, either not listening or pretending not to.

When Anne approached me to be my agent, she'd gone on and on about how it's my career and she would advise but didn't want to make decisions for me. I'd liked her because of all the people in Hollywood, she wasn't wrapped up in the money and status bullshit. She was one of the few true humans left in L.A. Now it sounds like she's swaying me in a definite direction. "Listen, Anne. It's *my* career. I—"

"I know. I tried to get you the audition. They told me thanks, but no thanks."

I freeze. "What? You mean, they already have someone in mind?"

"No. All the slots were taken."

I stiffen, trying to comprehend. In Broadway auditions, slots mean nothing. If a big enough name wants to get seen, they'll make the time to see him. Translation: They're really not interested. "Okay, but…"

"And Noah…" She's reluctant to say the next part, so I brace myself. "They also said they didn't think you were what they were looking for, for Roger."

What. The. Fuck. Roger is, essentially, me. The kid who's acutely aware of his own mortality and wants to make a meaningful mark on the world before he goes. "I don't get it. What do they mean by that?"

"The producer was familiar with your work and said they're looking for someone a little more…expressive. More passionate."

I drag a hand over my face. "Well I can understand that about my Megalith work. I mean, stone guys aren't passionate. But what about *Going Home*? And you know I've played Roger before…"

I trail off before *in college to rave reviews!* spills out of my mouth. Why don't I just drone on about the peanut butter commercial I did when I was twelve, while I'm at it?

For a fleeting moment, I step outside my body and see myself, sitting in an airport, fingers white-knuckling the phone. And I sense the way I must look to the whole fucking entertainment business. Desperate. Washed up. A joke.

"Noah. Of course I told him about *Going Home*. He was familiar with it. He said he didn't think you'd be right for the kind of Roger they were looking for. That's all." She pauses. "On the other hand, Bruce and the other guys at TriMast are chomping at the bit to work with you again."

I close my eyes, tight, until I see fireworks. "Yeah. I know."

Goddammit. Benedict Cumberbatch can be Dr. Strange and Alan Turing. Jennifer Lawrence can be Raven and win an

Oscar for *American Hustle.* Mark Ruffalo can be Bruce Banner and still keep churning out a healthy string of deep, indie roles.

I should fucking be able to do this.

"All right," I say. "Just keep me posted if anything else comes across your desk."

"I will, love," she says. "The car'll be around to pick you up at six a.m. sharp tomorrow. Keep me posted. Let me know when you land."

I end the call without responding. I grind my teeth. It takes all my energy not to launch the phone across the airport.

"Hey," Rebecca says next to me. "Was… Is everything okay?"

I stare straight ahead, willing myself to keep calm. "No. It's not."

I stand up and look at her. Her eyes are wide. "Why? What's happening?"

"It's more like, what's not happening," I mutter, grabbing my bag and my leather jacket. "I've got to go."

"Where? But…they're going to start boarding in less than an hour. Aren't you going to—"

"No. I'm not," I say. And I stalk off toward the airport exit.

I've got to get out of here, before I explode.

chapter fifteen

Becka

I promise, I didn't mean to eavesdrop.

But that's just what we writers do. We're curious people. We observe.

Also, sometimes we snoop. It's in our blood.

So I couldn't help it. He was right next to me, and so was the phone. And I pretty much heard everything his agent said to him, clear as day.

He has a contract in his hands that's worth fifteen million dollars, and I'm assuming it's to continue playing Megalith. But that isn't even the kicker.

The kicker is: *He doesn't even want it.*

He wants to do something real. Something meaningful. Something that showcases his abilities, and not his physique.

I'm trying to think how I would act in a similar situation. If I were a mega-bestseller in bodice-rippers, and yet I'd always wanted to write literary, but no one would give me a chance. Would I shun the bodice-rippers? Tell publishers to go to hell if they offered me a major contract?

Um…no. Because I would just be happy my stuff was being read.

But I don't have people judging my worth on how I look. For me, it's all about what is inside my head. And I'm so far below him, career-wise, I can't begin to understand what he's going through. For me, it'd be nice not to have to spend half of the month living on ramen noodles whenever my food budget gets tight.

Something tells me he doesn't have that problem, living in his mansion in Hollywood Hills.

I think about running after him, but I stop myself. He left me here because he wants to be alone.

I look at my phone and see a text from Bryn. ***Get your O?***

I sigh. I'm down to five percent charge. Just what I need, my phone to crap out now. But I need to talk to Bryn.

Me: ***Mission accomplished***

Bryn: ***Srsly? You beast! So you got a room with him?***

Me: ***Nope. Family restroom.***

Bryn: ***Aw, girl! Was it hot?***

Me: ***Beyond. But he's gone now. He left me. Story of my life.***

Bryn: ***What? Where did he go?***

Me: ***No clue. He got bad news from his agent and just took off.***

Bryn: ***NO! Go after him.***

Me: ***Why? I knew this was short-term to begin with.***

Bryn: ***This is why cell phones were invented. Long-distance relationships aren't ideal, but they happen.***

Me: ***I just… I think we both knew going into this that it was not going to last. And now he has other things on his mind. I get the feeling he thinks his career is falling apart.***

Bryn: ***Well, that's overdramatic. But I guess…he's an actor, so, makes sense… Go after him!***

Me: ***Can't! Flight is boarding in forty minutes!***

Bryn: ***GO. AFTER. HIM.***

I read her text over and over again.

Then my phone goes blank.

Shit. Charge, gone.

I wiggle my charger connections and let out a curse under my breath. Then I scan up and down the terminal. I don't see Noah anywhere.

And now I can't even text to tell him to get his ass over here.

Ripping my charger out of the wall, I lift my carry-on onto my shoulder and head out the way I saw him leave.

We might be only meant for these few hours in time. Or it could be just like he said. He's an actor. His business is bullshit. He specializes in making people believe things that aren't real. Maybe what we felt back there wasn't real.

But if he was acting, then he's the best actor in the world, and he deserves ALL THE ROLES. He shouldn't even have to audition. They should just throw parts his way.

I decide that if I can track him down, I'll tell him this. If I matter to him, then what I say will matter, too. If not, then… I guess what we had was meant to stay within these walls. Right now, I'm so tired, I'm running on adrenaline and can't even think straight.

I stop when I get to the TSA screening area. He's sitting at one of the benches there, where people usually put their shoes back on, elbows on his knees, chin resting on his fists. Staring at the arrivals boards.

I walk over to him and sit beside him.

"I'm stuck," he mumbles.

I shake my head. "No. Noah, don't you see? You're not. You may be Megalith, but that's not all you are. You are a great actor. You made a believer out of me. And you'll do it again. You just have to keep trying. Don't ever give up."

He looks at me, and for a moment I think he's going to tell me to go to hell. Then he smirks and says, "No. I'm literally stuck. Without my wallet, I can't go anywhere, unless I want to be fucked."

I let out a laugh. "Oh. Right. Where were you going to…"

"Just outside. To get some fresh air. Clear my head."

"Oh. Security line is long. You might have missed the flight if you did."

He shrugs. "You know. At this point, I don't know if that's such a bad thing." He looks down at his knees. "In less than twenty hours, I'm expected to sit in a make-up chair for four hours, getting made up for a photo shoot, where I have to pose and look menacing and…*fuck*."

He rakes both hands through his hair and tilts his face up to the ceiling, exhaling.

"I don't know if I can do it. I hate it. I don't know if I can play that game anymore."

I stare at him. "Oh, come on. Of course you can! Are you kidding me? Do you know how many actors out there would sacrifice a limb to be Megalith?" I jump to my feet and get on my soap box. "And do you know how many people actually love what they do for a living? Like, no one. Okay, maybe like five people on the face of the earth. But most of the time, it's just slogging through shit. I mean, I love writing, but most of the time when I'm writing, it's freaking *agonizing*. Work is not meant to be fun, which is why it's called work."

He's watching me, his eyes brooding and dark. I start to pace.

"And at least you're being compensated well. There's also the issue with me not making enough money and thinking every day that I might have to go and get a job at the local DQ because I can't make ends meet." I lift my hands to the sky. "So yes, while there's something to be said for shooting for the stars and doing what you love and not letting anyone tell you what to do, it doesn't mean flying out into space without a spacesuit. We're trained to look at what we don't have when we should be counting our blessings for what we do have."

He leans back in the chair, spreading his arms over the back of the chairs on either side of him. His voice is monotone. "Really."

He says it in a way that makes me think I've said something wrong. I stop. "Well, yes."

He stands up, comes so close to me it steals my breath. He reaches out, tangles his hand in my bun, pulling me to him.

"Is that what you think I'm doing? Flying without a spacesuit?"

Yes. I mean, no. I don't know. Who am I, again? I can't breathe. He's studying my features, so close, like he wants to devour them piece by piece.

"Has anyone ever told you that you have a nice ass, but doubted you can write? Even when you showed them you could?"

"No, but—"

"Again and again? Until there were absolutely no publishers left and you'd been completely locked out of the industry?"

"No, but—"

"Then you have no idea what's happening to me."

He lets my hair go and nudges me away from him, then has the gall to turn his back on me.

It fires me up.

Before I was annoyed at him. Now I'm getting downright pissed.

"Hey. Did you ever think that maybe you have a chip on your shoulder? That you're so worried people are going to judge you for your abs that you try too hard? I don't know… when I try to please people with my writing, I fail, because I don't write like *me*. Maybe all the comments about you being too wooden or not passionate enough…you should listen to them instead of blaming your abs, you son of a bitch."

He whirls on me, an incredulous look on his face. "So what are you saying? Are you saying it's not them…it's me?"

His gaze is bordering on rage-filled. But I won't back down on this. I thrust my chin out. "Yeah. Maybe it is."

He blows out a long breath of air, his eyes alight with rage. “Ridiculous,” he bites back.

We stare each other down. From the expression on his face, he’s clearly done with me. And I’m so done, too. Well, for now. If he put a hand out and grabbed a hold of me I’d let him take me anywhere.

I break his gaze first. “I’m going to go back to the gate. We’ll be boarding soon.”

He doesn’t make a move. He continues to give me that hard stare, lip curled up in a snarl, like he’s ready to fight.

I take a step toward the gate, and it hits me.

This could be the last time I ever see him.

Which is why I turn around. “Are you coming, or not?”

He’s silent for a long moment. And then he shakes his head.

No. I want to grab him. I want to drag him with me. Instead, I exhale. I nod. “I hope you find whatever it is you’re looking for,” I mumble, more to my chest than to him.

As I turn to leave, I know that it’s the end, and that this romance story can’t have a happy ending. It’s real life. *My* real life.

And I should’ve known better.

chapter sixteen

Noah

Of all the…fuck!

After Rebecca stalks away from me, whatever anger I had toward her morphs into disappointment with myself.

Because I know it even before she disappears from sight, down the busy corridor.

She's right.

I have been going into the auditions with a chip on my shoulder. At first, I was hopeful. I thought I was wanted and had the world at my feet. But as the audition opportunities stopped presenting themselves and I grew more and more desperate, I closed myself off. I got defensive. And now it shows in my readings.

Nobody wants a leading man who's an asshole.

And most of all, I was an asshole to her.

I regret that.

Because if anything could make the shit going on in my life better, it's her. The way she felt against me, the way she crawled under my skin and took hold…after we got out of that restroom, holding hands, I almost felt normal again. I almost felt like the old Noah Steele.

But this isn't the right time. I can't concentrate on her when my career is in a freefall.

Or is it? She's right about Megalith. He's not really a kiss of death. Maybe it's my attitude that's got me in this predicament. Maybe that's what needs the makeover.

I don't know. Fuck it.

I push my arms into my jacket, and as I do, I catch sight of a familiar face, near the duty-free shop.

It's the man in the tweed jacket, whom about a thousand years ago, Rebecca had said was a potential serial killer.

I watch him, skulking around, peering in a garbage can before stepping into the duty-free shop. How the fuck is he still here? Did he miss his flight, too? I find myself laughing bitterly.

Dammit. She's right about that, too. He does look like he's up to no good.

I should tell her that, too.

Hell. All these things that I want to tell her.

And yet my feet are rooted to the spot.

Trying to shake off the thought, I grab my phone and check it. The flight is probably in pre-boarding now. I should be heading over there.

I should bite the bullet, be a grown-up, and board the flight back to the town that hates me unless I'm in head-to-toe blue paint. Because this city isn't too fond of me, either. And yeah, work is work.

Rebecca's right about that, too.

Fuck. Why can't I get her out of my head?

As I'm thinking whether I should move, I see the bearded man in the tweed blazer grab the same perfume that Rebecca said she wore.

And wouldn't you know it?

He slips it into his pocket.

I lean forward, watching him. He strokes his beard as he studies a display of magazines at the exit of the shop, then easily skirts out of the doors. The cashiers don't notice. No one notices.

He's so professional. It's obvious he's done this before.

I recall what Rebecca said. *He should have Maximum Security stamped on his forehead.*

I search the concourse for someone in a security uniform, but there's never anyone like that nearby when you need one.

Lifting my bag onto my shoulder, I follow after him as he walks down the terminal, toward the gates, toting a beaten leather bag by a worn handle. I scan the tweed blazer, the bulge in the pocket that's the offending stolen item.

I fall in step, right behind him, and that's when it catches my eye.

Something in the small space under the flap of his case. It looks like the corner of a laptop.

A hot pink laptop.

chapter seventeen

Becka

I hate him.

How could I be so stupid?

Why am I a writer of romance books when I clearly can never get that part of my life right? Well, maybe it's like I was saying to him all along. Real life doesn't make good romance. Paris and making love in a luxurious penthouse, under the stars? That's what people want to read.

At least…

I blink out the memory of his mouth, hot on my skin, and storm down the concourse, a weight inside me as heavy as a stone.

I'm about to leave so much behind. And for once, I'm not thinking of the laptop. Those Ben and Leia stories sound just so trite now. My fingers have been itching to write because now, they think they can do better.

No. What I'm leaving behind is *him*. It was only fifteen hours, but in those hours, something happened.

It felt like Bitch Muse was not just waking up, but *on fire.*

So while maybe it was a mistake, wanting him, he was right. It's not the place, it's the person.

And it's not just my muse that wants him. As big of an asshole as he is, *I* still want him.

When I get to Gate 14, they're already boarding. The check-in counter attendant calls priority group three as I arrive. I check my ticket. I'm group nine.

I scan the concourse, hoping to see him. But he's not there.

It's at least fifteen minutes before the gate closes.

He can still make it.

He *has* to make it.

Because I don't know what I'll do if we leave things the way we did. Bitch Muse will never forgive my ass, that's for sure. I can see myself having writer's block until the day I die, an old, gray lady.

The attendant calls priority group four. More people begin to gather at the door, and the seats surrounding the gate start to empty out.

I wander over to the Hudson News to keep myself occupied. I need something for the flight, so I pick up the latest issue of *People*. I never read stuff like that, because I'm usually too busy writing. Or, trying to write.

As I'm standing on the check-out line, I glimpse the cover. There's a bubble on the corner that says, *Super Hot Hero Preview!* with a tiny picture of a bunch of superheroes underneath it, one of them slightly bluish and bulgy.

Oh, hell no.

The last thing I need to do on this flight is be greeted full-on by Megalith's abs, abs I was so close to, but never actually got to gaze at in full glory, because I had to settle for a family restroom instead of a hotel.

I shove the magazine back into the display and pick up a nice, safe copy of *Glamour*, instead.

Not that I give a shit about way overpriced new bikinis and making my bod beach-ready for the summer—as is made obvious by the king-size Snickers I also buy—but whatever.

When I pocket the candy bar and the magazine in my bag, I find that the area surrounding the gate is emptier still. The attendant is on priority group six. I crane my neck around the waiting crowds, hoping to see him, but I don't.

Shit. He's really not going to make this flight.

And Bitch Muse is saying, *Serves you right.*

chapter eighteen

Noah

"Hey!" I call to the man in the tweed jacket. "Stop!"

Without looking behind him, he starts to pick up his pace.

I break into a run, and so does he, dodging between travelers and tripping over rolling luggage as he heads down the concourse. I follow on his heels, grabbing the bag by the strap and pulling him to a stop.

"What the fuck do you think you're doing?" I demand.

"Unhand me," he says, pushing his glasses up on the bridge of his nose and scanning me with outrage.

"Hell, no. You're the bastard that took her laptop."

A heavyset woman in long braids approaches us. I look down and read the JFK Airport Security insignia on her jacket. "What seems to be the problem?" she asks, eyeing us both warily.

Before I can speak, the man blusters, "This man accosted me."

"Fuck that. You have a laptop that doesn't belong to you."

The woman crosses her arms and asks me, "Does it belong to *you*?"

"No. No it doesn't. But I bet you he has my wallet. That went missing, too."

The guard doesn't look surprised, like this kind of thing happens to her all the time. She wraps her hand around my upper arm, and does the same to the man. "All right. Why don't you two come with me?"

I plant my feet. "Why? Just look through his bag. And his jacket. He took a perfume bottle from the—"

"Sir," she says loudly, cutting me off. "Come. With. Me."

The man in the tweed jacket nods and says, "Certainly. I for one look forward to clearing my name of these accusations."

Like hell he does.

I punch my finger toward the gate, opposite the way she's trying to drag me. "Look. The woman who the laptop belongs to is about to get on the flight. She needs it. You should get this to—"

I stop and curse under my breath. She's not listening. She's radioing to someone else through a wireless on her lapel. "We have a situation here in front of Gate 2," she murmurs, clamping her hand harder on my arm. "And you're coming with me."

What the…? How the hell did I come out looking like the criminal in this situation?

I follow her down to the security office, getting looks from all the other travelers as we're joined by two other security guards. They take us into a back room behind the office where we'd filed the reports about our missing things and the young, pimply-faced officer tells us to sit down.

Then he leaves us alone.

I check my phone. The flight is scheduled to leave in fifteen minutes. The doors are probably closing soon.

And I don't want her to leave. I can't let her leave without telling her that she's right about me. About everything.

I've got to get there.

I start to pace. The man sits comfortably on the chair, legs crossed, hands folded over his knee, calm as can be, like he has nowhere to be. Scowling at him, I reach my hands up and touch the top of the door, hanging out of it, wondering how much longer this is going to take. The security guards are gathered around someone's cell phone. I think they're looking at a cat video.

Fucking hell.

"Hey." I wave at them. "Remember us?"

They trade glances, then the woman and the kid follow me into the room. "Okay, okay," the woman says, leaning on the jamb as I sit on the seat. "What's the issue here?"

The man says, "I have no issue. I bear no ill will toward anyone. I'm on a long layover from my trip to China. I was simply walking through the terminal, minding my own business. And this young man must have mistaken me for someone else, because he suddenly grabbed my bag and began hurling accusations."

"I was traveling with a woman," I explain. "She lost her laptop. She reported it, yesterday. It had a pink case. And when he walked by, I saw it in his bag."

The kid reaches into a file and pulls out the report. "Yeah. Here it is. A laptop reported missing last night, belonging to one Rebecca Stone."

She volleys a glance between us. "Is that so, now?" She motions to the man's bag. "Do you mind?"

He shakes his head, lifts the bag from the ground, and hands it to her, willingly offering himself up for search. How the hell is he going to explain this away?

She opens the flap and inspects the contents, then quirks an eyebrow at me. "You said a hot pink laptop?"

"Yeah, a MacAir." It occurs to me from the way she's looking inside, moving things around, that it's not there. It was too obvious before. I jump to my feet, peer inside, and sure enough…fucking hell.

No. I saw it. There was definitely something hot pink in his bag. And now it's gone.

I whirl to him. "What the fuck did you…"

I stop. I look at my own bag, just as the female guard gets the same idea and steps around the table, reaching for it.

It looks a little more…overstuffed than usual.

How the hell…

It suddenly occurs to me. Impatient dumbass that I was, I'd turned my back on him and my bag long enough to ask the security guards what was taking too long.

She unzips my bag and frowns as she raises her eyes to meet mine. "Well, well, well. Would you look at that?"

She reaches into my carry-on and pulls out the laptop and the perfume, and sets them on the table, to taunt me.

To twist the knife harder, the man next to me gasps in surprise.

And I thought *I* was the actor.

Did I mention how much I fucking hate this city?

chapter nineteen

Becka

I grab my phone, hoping it has some charge left so that I can text Noah and tell him to get his ass to the gate.

When I try to turn it on, it doesn't respond.

The attendant calls for priority group eight.

Hell. Now it's too late for me to go after him.

He's really okay with ending it like this.

I guess I should be, too.

But I'm not.

I wander up to the podium where two attendants are standing, one scanning tickets as people head down the platform to the airplane.

"Excuse me," I ask the other. "Someone was supposed to board. I think he's in the terminal but I don't see him here. Noah Steele?"

She lifts her phone. "Would you like me to page him?"

I nod.

She speaks in monotone into the phone, her voice echoing above us. "Noah Steele, please proceed to Gate 14. Your flight is boarding. Noah Steele, please proceed to Gate 14."

She hangs up and sees me still standing there, clutching the podium for dear life.

"Is there something else I can help you with?"

"No…well, yes, actually. How much longer before the doors close?"

She surveys the line. "Oh, I'd say not more than five, ten minutes."

"And if people don't show up?"

"Once we've called all the priority groups, if someone hasn't shown up, we'll begin assigning those seats to our standby list. It's a full flight. We have a few people on standby."

I frown and push away from the podium. "Thank you."

I scan the terminal again. Then I reach into my bag and grab the roll of butter rum Life Savers. I suck one into my mouth, hoping it'll calm me down.

It doesn't work.

Damn you, you stubborn son-of-a-bitch. Get your ass on this plane.

"Priority group nine," the attendant behind me calls.

Shit.

chapter twenty

Noah

"Goddammit, he planted that on me," I mutter as the three guards eye me up and down like I'm a piece of trash. "Don't you see that?"

Clearly, they don't. The guy is sitting beside me, quietly stroking his chin and reading a beaten copy of Proust. He probably only looks suspicious to people like Rebecca.

If I had Rebecca here, she'd set them straight.

The kid says to him, "Sorry, sir. This'll just be a moment, and we'll have you on your way. We need your statement for the report."

"No trouble at all," the man says, not looking up from his book.

I let out a disbelieving groan. What a cocksucker. "So what's going to happen?"

"We'll file our report, and you'll be turned over to the NYPD."

"The NYPD…" I repeat, hardly able to believe what I'm hearing. "You've got to be shitting me. I didn't do this. *He* did." I jab a finger at him. "I don't even have a record."

"All right, all right," the kid mutters, grabbing a chair and sitting across from me with a laptop. "You have a driver's license?"

"No," I mutter, shoving my hands deep into the pockets of my jacket and slumping far into the chair.

"No?"

I look over at the professor over there, nose buried in a book. "Ask him. He probably took my wallet."

Professor looks up. "I'm at a loss for words. Truly."

The kid scowls at me. "You know. It doesn't help your case any to have an attitude. What's your name?"

"But this is ridiculous. I didn't steal—"

"Save it for court. Name?"

I frown. It's suddenly getting hot in here. I tear off my jacket and throw it over the back of the chair. "Noah. Noah…" I lower my voice. "Stipplethorpe."

And I spell it, since no one in the free world knows how to spell that last name.

The kid's hands race over the keyboard. "Address?"

"7689 Mulholland Drive, Hollywood Hills, California," I mutter.

"Swanky. What are you doing stealing laptops?" he says, not looking at me.

"I didn't. Like I've been trying to—"

"Phone?"

I answer that question, as well as the dozens that follow it, regarding my medical history, HIV status, whether I think I'll harm myself, all the while realizing that not only am I going to miss my flight, not only am I going to lose the girl… I'm going to spend the next day in jail.

My mother's going to have a coronary when she finds out.

I scrape a hand over my face as I suddenly hear the faraway announcement over the intercom. "Noah Steele, please proceed to Gate 14."

"Not that you care. But they're calling for me," I tell him, pointing at the speaker. "My flight is leaving."

He stops typing to listen to the rest of the announcement. Then he shrugs. "Yeah. I don't care." He types some more and then stops. "Wait… Steele? You said your last name was… Stipplethorpe."

"My legal name is. Steele is my stage name."

"Gotcha." He keeps typing. "So profession…actor?"

I narrow my eyes at him. "Or criminal mastermind. Take your pick."

"Actor." He types some more. Then he finishes and starts to read back the report to himself, his lips moving slightly. He makes a correction, and frowns. "So you were taking a flight back to LAX, huh?"

"Yep."

He backs away from the computer. "Okay. Wait right here."

He leaves. The woman with braids comes back and says, "I notified the police." She scowls at me and smiles at the professor. "I'm sorry for the trouble. Can we get you some coffee?"

For fuck's sake.

He shakes his head. "I would like to make my statement and be off. My flight's leaving soon."

She nods. "Right away, sir. Come with me, please."

He begins to stand, giving me a curt nod. Fucker.

As he does, the acne-faced kid appears in the door, looking like he just saw a ghost. "Wait… Noah Steele?"

"Yeah?"

A look of awed delight dawns on his face, kind of like a kid at Christmas. "Holy shit. You're him. You're Megalith."

chapter twenty-one

Becka

I approach the doors slowly, so I am truly the last person who is going to board the airplane.

I always used to get annoyed when people held up flights. But here I am, dragging my feet.

I grab my phone in my sweaty hand, trying to get the screen to activate, and then realize. "Oh. Geez. My boarding pass is on my phone. And my phone just died," I say, biting my lip.

"Not a problem," the woman says. "ID?"

I pull out my driver's license and hand it to her, thinking this is a brilliant way to stall for time.

But it only buys me a couple of seconds. She prints out a new one, scans it, and hands it to me. "Enjoy your flight."

I hesitate there, my pulse beginning to pound in my throat. Take one last look down the concourse, looking for his scrumptious sandy head. "Um…"

"Yes?"

And that's when it starts to happen. My vision starts to blur, and my hands start to shake. Oh no.

The last time I had a panic attack, I'd had Noah to catch me. Now, I feel so alone. I blink furiously, trying to calm myself down. But my heart is shuddering in my chest.

Oh god. Oh god.

"Miss? Are you all right?"

"Water. I need some water…" I croak out.

I hear the woman calling for someone as everything goes dark around me. I feel myself sinking into a hole as someone brings a cup of water to my lips. I take a sip.

Open my eyes. Fluorescent light assaults me.

"Miss. Are you all right to board?"

I look up and see the attendant, as well as a bunch of other employees, crowding around me. "Um. You have people on standby for this flight?"

She nods.

"If I wanted to take the next flight…to Austin…when would that be?"

She types on the keyboard. "Oh. Not until tomorrow afternoon, unfortunately."

I gnaw on my lip. "Would there be a charge?"

"Miss. I've already taken your ticket. You've already checked in…are you able to board this flight or not?"

I suck in a breath as two men help me to my feet to an audience of onlookers, some concerned, some just nosy. The room wavers, but as I blink, everything becomes clearer. I slowly let go of the men's arms and stand on my own.

This is stupid. Why am I waiting for him? He's a big-ass movie star with a big-ass ego and abs the entire female population drools over, and the last time he looked at me it was as if he never wanted to see me again. If we were meant to happen, he'd be boarding this flight with me.

I should be happy to get as far away from him as possible.

Ecstatic.

The attendant is waiting for me, her hand out, ushering me down the platform to the plane.

I nod at her and swallow back the panic inside me. "Thank you."

And I head through the door and down the gangway.

chapter twenty-two

Noah

"Holy shit. I love that part. Where you rip the guy's head off and then say, 'Guess I'm ahead now.' Classic."

I smile as I sign another autograph, my hand growing numb. "Thanks, man."

Turns out, all three security guards are *huge* Galaxy Titans fans. Acne-kid, whose name is Brandon, is the biggest fan of them all, randomly reciting every one of my twelve lines from the past six movies, as he kneels in front of me in worship.

Once they found out who I was, the tide shifted. They nearly tackled the professor to the ground and bull-whipped him into another room. I haven't seen him since.

So, being a superhero does have its privileges. Turns out, I could've murdered a bunch of people and they'd still think I was pretty cool.

Now, I'm surrounded by a small sea of admirers, all wanting selfies and autographs. The security guards told some other people in TSA, and now it's like a swarm of locusts. They're gathering around me, smiling, hugging me, and great as it is, all I can think is…the flight. I'm missing the flight.

"Hey, man," Brandon says as he takes his twelfth selfie with me. "Can you make that face? That grrrrr face, you know? Pose like him. You know, flex your muscles?"

I nod, assume the pose I'm undoubtedly going to have to make for three hours straight during the publicity photos, with my biceps on display, and he takes another shot. "That's one for my Facebook profile pic."

"Yeah, um…listen. My flight? I really would like to get the laptop back to its rightful owner."

"Right. Right," he says, handing me the laptop. "Sorry we couldn't find your wallet. Anyway, I'll escort you there so you don't have any trouble."

I check my phone. "Can you radio someone to hold the flight, or something? It's going to leave in a few minutes, you know."

"We can't, but… No problem, man. I got this," he tells me, slapping me on the shoulder. He clears his throat and calls, "Okay, guys. Party's over. Clear an aisle. Megalith has to get to his flight."

Slowly, the sea of people parts, and I make my way down the narrow pathway, shaking hands and taking selfies. When we step out of the security office, people swing their heads toward me. I fasten the baseball hat back on my head, but not everyone in the airport gets a security guard escort. They're looking at me like, *Which important person is he?*

The kid lopes along, too slow for my liking. I glance at my phone again. "Look. My flight's leaving in two minutes."

I break into a run, tearing off through the sea of people, Brandon on my heels. It's a mad dash, but by now I hear people whispering my name. Whispering *Megalith.* Word about me has spread like wildfire, unbelievably. Gate 14 comes into view, and I dodge people standing still and hurdle over rolling luggage, skidding to a stop in front of the door.

Breathing heavy, I fall to a crouch, shaking my head, fisting handfuls of my hair.

Behind me, Brandon stops abruptly on the tile, then lets out a breathless, "Aw, shit."

The doors are closed.

Through the window, I watch yet another plane pulling away from the gate, without me.

chapter twenty-three

Becka

"I'm so sorry," I tell the check-in attendant as she walks me up the gangway. "You see, I decided… I'm a writer. And this story is only half-written. I can't leave just yet. Not until I know for sure how things turn out. Right?"

She just rolls her eyes like, *I don't want to hear it, crazy writer woman.* She pushes open the door to the airport terminal and I let out the first relaxed breath I have in hours.

I don't know why. I'm back in hell. Nowhere near home. But something tells me this is right where I should be.

"Let's see about getting you on another flight," she mutters, directing me to the podium. "Tomorrow afternoon?"

"Yes. Thank you," I say, shaking, babbling. "I left something very important here, and I can't go until I make sure—"

"Rebecca?"

My heart seizes in my chest. I whirl.

Noah.

He's standing there, baseball cap down over his eyes, out of breath, looking like a fucking dream. Brock has never looked so good.

He came back.

He came back, for me.

"I think I missed the flight."

I bring my hand to my mouth because I think I might sob. I will not do that, though. I refuse to. "I did, too."

Then my eyes trail down to something stuffed under his arm.

My hot pink laptop.

No. I will not cry. I will not will not will not.

But my face must crumple a little, because he says, "Hey. All's good, right? The very important thing you left is right here."

I shake my head. "The very important thing I left was *you.*"

He takes my face in his hands, tilting my chin up to his mouth, and kisses me. Just kisses and kisses me and everything falls away.

When I break the kiss, I ask, "Where did you find it?"

He laughs, low and sexy. "Long story."

"Well, guess what? I have until tomorrow afternoon to hear it."

He presses his forehead against mine. "If you think I'm going to spend the next day in this hellhole, you are out of your mind."

"It's not the place. It's the person," I murmur.

He laughs, sexy and low, so it vibrates deep inside me. "Ok. I'll admit. *Sometimes* it's the place."

"Hotel?" I ask.

He nods.

"But…you can't leave the secure area. If you leave, you may be stuck in New York for days. You don't have your wallet."

"I don't fucking care." He kisses me again. Hungrily. "I want you. There's a hotel in NoMad that holds rooms for Tri-Mast. We'll get a room there. And I'll work out the lost wallet thing later."

My knees wobble as I stare into his eyes. "Okay. Let's do it."

Then I break from him, holding his hand tight in mine, and see a security guard and the check-in counter attendant staring at us, looking vaguely embarrassed to have witnessed our PDA.

But I can't say I regret it. Hell no, it's the opposite of regret.

Everything after that happens in one, horny blur. The two of us, switching our tickets to the following day (again). Us rushing, hand in hand, out past security, into the cab line, finally taking our first breaths of fresh, outdoor air in a day. His solid hand on the small of my back, guiding me into the taxi, barking out, "NoMad" before fastening his mouth onto mine.

We make out like kids, like we're starved of each other, groping and feeling and sucking and touching, and oh my god, his tongue is hot and sweet. I don't need air because I'm feeding off of him. His hands are everywhere, pulling me to him like he never wants to let me go again.

There may or may not have been traffic, but it seems like we pull up in front of the hotel in two seconds flat. I hand over my credit card to pay, knowing I'm flushed all over.

He guides me inside this monstrous, swanky-looking hotel, looking way more comfortable here than I ever will. I should probably tell him that for all my bluster about sexy Ben, the richest place I've ever stayed at is a Holiday Inn Express on the Interstate during family vacations. He may not be wearing a suit, but he clearly belongs here. He speaks with the man at the front desk, who gives him a warm greeting, and a moment later, he's back with me, holding a key card.

And his hand goes right to the small of my back again. This time, stroking it, making my insides bubble with need.

We get to the bank of elevators; he presses the UP button several times, as if that will make the elevator come faster. "Nervous?" he whispers in my ear.

I probably should be. After all, this is Megalith. The man of stone abs. The guy with the gorgeous face that made me swoon the fifty-seven times I watched *Going Home* on Netflix.

"No," I tell him. And I mean it. Just unbelievably horny. My panties feel soaked between my thighs.

After a tinny ding, the gilded doors open to an empty elevator. He guides me inside, pressing the button for the floor.

When the doors slide closed, he corners me against the gleaming mirrored walls, caging me there. Foreheads pressed together, he stares intently into my eyes. "God, I want you so bad."

"I'm right here," I whisper. "Just take me."

"Here?" He raises an eyebrow. "Last I heard, you weren't into the PDA."

"I may have changed my tune."

He lowers his mouth onto mine and kisses me. The kisses just get better and better. He sucks my tongue and in the mirrored walls I catch glimpses of my hands splayed upon his strong back. I feel my nipples pebbling and while I might have never been into the PDA before, at this moment I don't think I would mind if he took me in the middle of Times Square.

The elevator finally opens, and he guides me to the room, waving the card in front of the panel on the door. He pushes it open and stands aside to let me go in first. I flip on the lights, and I gasp. It's enormous. "Are you freaking kid—"

And then I'm gasping again because the door clicks closed and he cages me against the walls, vising my wrists above my head as he puts his hot, open mouth on my neck.

Holy god.

He threads his fingers through my hair, ripping out the tie, letting my hair fall on my shoulders, veiling my face. Then he breaks his assault on my neck to behold his creation.

"Holy shit, you have the sexiest hair. Just like that. Falling in your face like that. Fuck, you're a goddess."

I need him inside me again. Everything he does and says only makes the obsession stronger.

He places his finger on my cheek and runs a sinuous trail downward, to my jaw, and then my throat, his eyes following that same trail, slowly, steadily. The act of breathing escapes me.

Still holding my wrists, he walks me backward, toward the enormous bed. He sits on the very edge of the bed, so that he's lower than me.

Then he grasps my chin in his hand, dragging me down to his level. Opening my lips wide and thrusting his tongue inside, he claims my mouth, owning it and every part of me.

As he flicks his tongue inside my mouth, he tugs my shirt. Popping it over my head, he buries his face between my breasts, tugging the fabric down, kissing the swell of my breasts.

Then he brings his hands over my shoulders, looking at me fully. He gazes at my breasts with raw hunger before rolling my bra down over my already hardened nipples.

He cups one in his hand, rubbing the pad of his thumb over one engorged nipple. The other slips behind my back, and he easily unclasps the bra. He eases the straps down my arms, and I shrug off my bra.

He molds my breasts together and lets out a guttural sound that tells me he approves. He licks the nipple, lightly at first, and then fastens his mouth on it, sucking, doing a circular motion with his tongue. I growl.

He wraps his strong arms around my waist, cocooning me within his warm, perfect muscles. Meanwhile, he continues his assault on my breasts, licking, sucking, driving me insane.

Then he edges back farther onto the bed, sitting back, and pulls me onto his lap, straddling his jeans. He erection, hard and insistent, presses through the stiff material, into the V of my panties…a straight shot into my core. I wriggle atop his hardness, feeling it go deeper, and he groans.

"Have you any idea what you're doing to me, Rebecca?" he rasps out.

Rebecca. No one calls me that. And no man has ever called me that during sex.

He kisses me again. Harder. Deeper. Deeper than I ever thought possible. The stubble on his jaw from a few days unshaven is a welcome pain, rubbing my chin raw. I straddle him, thighs spread wide over him, his hands jammed under my ass, caressing it, thumb lightly rubbing its way up my slit.

His pupils are dilated, his eyelids heavy, he licks torturously at my lips and grinds his erection into me. "Goddamn, Rebecca, you're so beautiful. You feel perfect."

He crushes his mouth onto me, and in a blink, he lifts me up and nudges me back onto the bed, kissing my ear with a hot breath. He lifts me up by the arms, gently resting my head down so that my head is upon the pillow. His mouth sinks into the skin on my neck, biting and tasting as he delivers nibbling kisses to the hollow of my throat. Meanwhile, his hand slips its way over my breasts, down my torso, over my abdomen. I arch to his touch, pushing my center up to him, wanting his hands lower, between my legs.

But he doesn't go there. I spread my legs, wanting him desperately, but he's teasing me again. "Don't tease me," I breathe out. "Not now."

"I'm not allowed to?" he murmurs, licking his way down my throat. "I won the hunt."

At first I think, *What hunt?* And then I remember. The laptop. And who cares if I lost? All is right with the world. I have my laptop back and I'm being worshipped by a gorgeous man. But then it hits me. "You didn't win. You didn't get the Texas license."

"Ah. You're right," he rasps out, kissing the tip of my chin. His eyes are heavy and dark, almost black in the bare daylight silhouetting the blackout curtains. "Put my hand where you want it."

I take his hand and guide it, over my abdomen, between my legs. His fingers flirt lightly with the barely-there fabric. Finally, he lifts the thin strap of my thong, and delves inside, palming my sex, his fingers tangling in the fine, curly hairs there. He strokes it gently, not invasively, just barely, as if cautiously asking for the invitation to proceed.

I can't help it. I can feel myself becoming unhinged, losing control. I spread my legs apart slightly, giving him silent approval.

He presses his fingers deeper between my legs, stroking my mound as he kisses me. I run my hands up his rock-hard chest, down to his abs, feeling the ridges there.

Ohmigod. He's like a solid, rippling wall.

I don't know if I'm ready to see this.

I must tremble, or my eyes must widen. Something gives me away. Because he lets out a chuckle. "Don't worry. I assure you. I'm mortal."

He rolls onto his elbow, lifting the shirt up over his head with one hand and pulling it over his head.

And holy fucking shit. CGI nothing. I've never seen such a perfect human chest before, even on the cover of a magazine. I gaze at it, wondering what devil he sacrificed his soul to in order to achieve that.

It doesn't deter him in the least. He crawls next to me, spreading my legs, nudging my thong aside, all the while staring at my face. Without hesitation, he walks his fingers over my wet folds and brushes a knuckle over my clit, eliciting a groan from me. As soon as he does that, he inserts a finger inside me.

I moan out all the breath in my lungs.

He feasts on my nipples again, licking them more, as I arch and buck against his mouth. He withdraws a finger from me, only to press it back in a moment later. Kissing, nibbling, licking, and fucking me with his fingers. I move in rhythm with him, gasping.

Suddenly, he sits back. My clit misses the attention instantly, but before I can totally crumble, he ups the ante.

"Come here," he growls from the end of the bed, his hands twining around the globes of my ass, squeezing them. He grips my ass tight and easily slides me to the edge of the bed. I draw in a sharp breath as he kneels between my thighs, spreading them.

I struggle onto my elbows as he bends in front of me, his eyes trained on my clit. The thought of his tongue on me makes every nerve in my body sizzle with electricity.

"I need to taste you, Rebecca. I've been thinking about it since the moment we met," he murmurs.

He bends his head and licks his way up my thigh. He pauses to nudge aside my thong, his breath on me enough to send me soaring into oblivion. When his tongue gently touches the sensitive nub, I arch up and let out a cry.

"Oh, my god," I groan as his tongue circles my clit, making me writhe on the bed. I buck in time to his lapping, spreading my legs apart. Wider and wider, shamelessly. My dignity has long since stopped mattering.

And then, just when I'm positive it can't get any better, it does. He inserts a curled finger into my pussy, pumping it slowly in and out, once, twice…

And I completely lose it. I throw myself over the edge, thrashing and screaming, biting my fist hard.

"God," I moan, shattered to pieces, filled with liquid heat and electricity, so hot I can barely breathe. I scream as I grind myself shamelessly against his mouth.

"You taste as delicious as I thought you would," he says, lifting up off the bed, the stubble around his mouth wet with my juices. I'm still shaking, my body feeling boneless, like a pile of jelly. I think I can die now and be happy.

He stands there as I come down, smiling smugly at me, knowing just what an amazing piece of work he is. I'm trying to figure out how it came to this, me, here, with Brock. Megalith. I can't stop drinking his body in with my eyes. God, he's not built like a stone mountain, which is probably where the CGI comes in…but he is cut. Ridiculously cut and tanned and…

My eyes trail up to his throat, and that's when I see it.

Tied on a leather cord, around his neck.

A small white thing, capped in silver.

A shark's tooth.

A fucking shark's tooth.

My jaw drops. I point.

He nods. He unbuckles his pants, shimmies them over his hips, stands, and slides them off, then crawls onto the bed beside me, completely naked.

And I really think I might die.

Oh, god. He's perfection, head to toe.

"All right," he murmurs, dipping his head to kiss my nipple again. "*You* win. What would you wish of me, Rebecca?"

If I weren't already nearly naked on the bed next to him, writhing for his touch, I might have run away. But I'm too invested now. That, and too fucking horny.

I had wishes. Lots and lots of wishes. I'd been turning them around and around in my head. But right now, only one wish comes to mind. It escapes my mouth before I can even really think. "I want you inside me."

He sweeps a shock of his sandy hair aside on his forehead, then reaches down and very slowly drags a finger over my hip, plucking up the strap of my thong and taking it down. He slips it over my hips, down my thighs, and slowly lifts one leg, then the other, removing it entirely and casting it aside.

He lies on his back and hooks a finger at me. "I want you on top of me, so I can see you."

Gladly. I sit up, sliding half of the way, dropping a knee on the other side of his hips. He scoops a hand around my waist and drags me up onto his middle. Up there, atop him, I feel his cock pressing urgently into my sex.

He sweeps his eyes over my face, down to my breasts. He places a hand on each of my hips. "Ready?"

I nod.

Hand splayed on my waist, he applies pressure at my hips as I slide onto him. His tip touches my folds, and I adjust my bottom on top of him, finding the right place to sink into. I let out a gasp as I start to slip onto him.

My eyes hold his, widening as I take him in, feeling myself stretch all the more. He's so long, hard, and so, so alive inside me. Eyes fastened on mine, he brings his hands up my sides, to my breasts, rubbing my nipples with the pads of his thumbs.

I moan softly as I take the last of him in.

"Is this everything you wished for?" he asks, and now one of his hands is by my face, twisting a lock of my hair.

I nod, settling down onto him, feeling him so deep inside me, my thighs spread upon his hips. "More."

He slides his hands under my ass and lifts me up. Then he groans and sits up, twisting my hair at the nape and grabbing it in two vicious handfuls as he rocks into me. I'm the one on top, but he's controlling this ride, pushing into me, setting the rhythm. I let him. Whatever he is doing, he is doing it damn right, striking a chord in me that has never been hit before. I feel it with every thrust. Deeper, deeper. All I have to do is wrap my arms tight around his back, settle into the rhythm, and let him take me there.

And damn. He gets me there in record speed. The friction against my clit spirals out to my extremities, turning my entire body into a bundle of nerves. Every time he rocks his hips into me, it only goes deeper.

He drags his hands down so they're spanning my waist as he drills into me, watching my breasts sway to the rhythm. The look on his face is deliciously raw and intense, a sheen of sweat on his forehead, the tendons in his neck tight. He guides me up and down, again and again, faster, faster, until the bed's shaking and the headboard pounding against the wall.

I run my hand down his smooth, work-of-art chest. He has just a smattering of hair on his pectorals, and now, it's damp and dark with sweat. I let my mouth wander, hot and wet, over his skin, sucking and licking and thrashing on him as we move more and more erratically. My fingernails claw at his back and my teeth dig into his shoulder, tasting his perfect salty sweetness.

One moment we're fucking and biting and moving and growling, and the next moment, he's shuddering in me, cock jerking inside me, our wet bodies fused together with sweat. As he comes, I feel myself flying over that edge, soaring and releasing all the tension inside of me in endlessly rolling waves.

Coming. I'm coming again. Harder than last time, a thousand times harder.

Holy shit.

He lets out a groan, tensing as he holds onto me, gripping me in his slick hands, his head falling onto my shoulder. I come and come and come, every pore in my body screaming out a release so intense that I can't keep my body from trembling. As he comes, he rolls me over, murmuring words I can't quite make out as he thrusts into me, ever deeper.

Then he pulls out of me, rolling onto his back, and stares at the ceiling. "Now that's what I call a layover."

I laugh at him as he rolls back onto his elbow and raises an eyebrow at me, eyes gleaming.

He runs a finger down my breastbone, to my abdomen, making me shiver and giggle before the beginnings of desire intercede. His smile fades, and I know he's thinking of it, too.

We're both dead tired. But from the look in his eyes, I don't think we'll be doing much sleeping.

And I wouldn't have it any other way.

chapter twenty-four

Noah

I nod off for about three minutes, and when I wake, Rebecca is lying on her stomach next to me, her pink laptop open, typing away.

"The bitch muse has fallen in line?" I ask, running a hand up the back of her thigh, to where it meets her ass.

"I think so," she murmurs, tapping her chin thoughtfully. "I think a lot of this, I need to delete."

"Why?"

"It's not as good as I thought it was."

"Hell, no. Let me read some of it."

She looks back at me, her hair falling in her eyes, and it's so sexy that my cock twinges right away for her. "Are you sure?"

"Yeah. Give me a juicy part, though. The penthouse suite, under the stars."

"Mmmm…okay," she says reluctantly, scrolling as I grab my reading glasses from my carry-on and slide next to her, on my stomach. She stops and looks at me. "I didn't know you wore glasses."

I put them on. "Only sometimes. I've worn the shit out of my contacts."

"They make you look hot. Like Clark Kent."

"You *had* to mention superheroes?" Giving her a doubtful look, I pull the laptop toward me and read: *My body is trembling from head to toe as the elevator stops at the top floor and the doors open to his penthouse suite. I know that whatever happens, I'm not going to leave here a virgin. Ben is in love with me. I can't possibly resist this man any longer…*

Rebecca is clearly talented. I can see that from the first line. Leia is kind and thoughtful and doesn't think enough of herself, so I can see where she's similar to Rebecca. She lets Ben take charge. And Ben…he's kind of an asshole.

Or it might just be that I hate the thought of any other man being with Rebecca.

"So, she's a virgin?"

"Well…yes."

"How old is she?"

"Twenty-four, I think?" When I give her a look, she gets defensive. "What?"

"Nothing. Wow," I murmur as I read. "This part is good. He pulls one little string on her dress and she's completely naked. I like that. You should dress like that."

I look back at her, and she's chewing nervously on her lower lip. "Well, he told her not to wear underwear. So he's kind of been…playing with her, under the table. All through dinner."

"Ah. That's hot." I read more. It suddenly occurs to me. "Dinner…in Paris?"

She nods.

"And then a seven-hour flight back to his home in New York? That's a lot of…build-up."

"No. Actually, he has a penthouse in Paris, too."

"Oh. Of course." So Leia is standing in front of him, in a thong and high heels. She's trembling, looking up at him after a sumptuous dinner in Paris, and tells him she wants to be made love to, on the patio, under the stars. He scoops her up and lays her body down on the chaise lounge outside.

"High heels. Gets me every time," I breathe out. Then I read more…and I lose myself. Because this girl—Leia—is doing things that no virgin in history has ever done.

It's good…it's dirty. And it's getting my cock hard. Not because of the words but because I know that this shit went through the mind of the sweet little girl next to me.

Rebecca clearly has a very vivid imagination. Or… "Is any of this from experience?"

She shakes her head. Her cheeks are pink. "Is it terrible?"

"No, it's…fucking hell." I read more. Hell, I can't stop reading. "We should reenact this part. For research purposes. Just so you make sure you get it exactly right."

She smiles and studies the screen. "Which part?"

"This one. On the lounge. I want to do this."

She reads it over. "It's still daytime. There are no stars."

"Fuck it. I want you again. Any way I can have you." I scoop the laptop up and lay it on the ground, then lift her by the waist and roll her atop me. I clench her tight and push her tits against my chest as I kiss her.

"I want to take a shower first," she says, squirming out of my grip. I reach for her, but she scuttles away. "I feel gross."

I roll onto my elbow, defeated. "Yeah. That was just what I was going to say. You feel gross."

She grabs a pillow and throws it at me. "Unless you want to take one with me?"

She doesn't have to ask twice. In a split second, I'm in the bathroom. I open the glass door and run the water in the stall shower, extra hot.

She comes in and gazes around in awe. "This shower is bigger than some small countries."

I rip the paper on a travel-size bar of soap. "Get in. Consider it research."

Steam wafts all around us, casting everything in a hazy, dreamlike state. She steps in, and water immediately soaks her hair, darkening it brown. Water trickles over her curves, and her nipples go hard as rocks.

My cock twinges again for her. She looks incredible, the water glistening on all her naked parts.

"Turn around. You're really gross. That means you need a thorough cleaning."

I step in beside her and roll the soap in my palms, under the water. I begin to lather her skin. I wash her back thoroughly, taking care not to miss a single spot. Over her fragile shoulder blades, down the small of her back, up and down each thigh, slipping my fingers between the crack of her ass, making her moan.

Even when she's clean, I can't stop myself.

She squirms for me, as I run my soaped-up hands up and down her chest, and she's clearly enjoying it from the groans she lets out. Her nipples are so hard, and her eyes are closed, and more than once she has to brace herself against the tile wall. She throws her wet hair over her shoulder and gives me a sexy pout as I press my fingers between her legs and kiss her neck. "Am I clean yet?"

"Not yet. Getting there."

She motions for the soap. "Give it, dude."

I hand it to her. She starts to lather me up, her hands moving slickly over my body. Goddamn, her fingers are magic. When she reaches for my cock, it's already rock hard again.

Her hands are moving harder, faster on me. I tilt my head back, savoring the feeling of her running her wet hands over my body. "I'm really gross, too."

She lathers the soap more and smiles at me. "Oh. Disgusting."

I hold up my hands. "Feel free to spend as much time as you need. I understand the importance of good research."

And she does. She lathers me so good, not missing a spot of skin, so that when she finishes and inspects me, my cock is raging for her. I pull her to me so fast that the soap slips from her hands.

I slam my mouth on hers, kissing her hard as the water rains down at us. Her skin's slick, but I hold her immobile, pressing her tits against my chest.

Then I whirl her back to me, so she's facing the shower wall. I wedge my knee between her thighs, forcing her to part her legs.

Bending my frame over her, I spread kisses over her back, tossing her wet hair over her shoulder, my hands curved around her front, kneading her breasts, finding those hard nipples. She leans over, lifting her ass to me, guiding my cock to her entrance.

In answer, I thrust into her with no hesitation as she presses her palms against the shower wall. The steam from the shower swirls around us as I fuck her from behind, slow, steady, her body rocking back and forth to meet me.

"God, Noah," she moans, and I don't think I'd ever heard my name sound sweeter than when it came from her mouth, when she was lost in the throes of passion. "Please don't stop."

I don't. I thrust into her, tightening my hands on her hips and drawing her closer to me, smashing her onto my cock. She screams out her release, and I find it again only a second later, as our bodies continually meet in an explosion of heat and desire. My whole body pulsates and I growl as I unleash myself into her, breathing hard.

I thought one night in a hotel with her, fucking her senseless, would cure myself from wanting her.

But now I know that isn't the case.

I only want her more.

chapter twenty-five

Becka

After I get out of the shower, I put on one of Noah's t-shirts, then open up the blinds in the sitting area, sit at the dining table, and start to write.

And I write. And I write.

And holy god, it's some of my best shit, ever.

I can no longer call my muse a bitch.

Some time later, Noah comes out, freshly shaved, damp hair slicked back, a towel slung loosely over his hips.

He's innocently brushing his teeth, but the man is made of sex. I could write pages just on the way he looks, his broad frame filling the door. The damp hair on his pectorals pointing the way down to his…

"Hey. Author girl. Are you hungry?"

That snaps me out of my sexually-charged trance. Author girl? I've always considered myself a writer, but author seemed too pretentious for a girl who'd never had shit published.

I smile. "Thirsty, mostly."

We'd gone through the two bottles of Evian they'd put on the counter. Noah checks the mini-fridge. "No more water. Coke?"

I shake my head.

He picks the room service menu off the table and hands it to me. "Get what you want. They'll bill it to the room and TriMast can take care of it."

I don't want to bother the hotel workers just for a stupid bottle of water. I scan around for my carry-on. "I think I saw a vending machine with water at the end of the hall."

I grab for my carry-on and start to sort through everything in there, looking for the quarters that always inevitably fall to the bottom of the bag. I get seventy-five cents when my hand wraps around something rectangular and smooth and… I have no idea what it can be.

I reach in and pull out a wallet.

Not my wallet, though.

"Oh, my god."

Noah's eyes fall on it and glimmer with recognition. He laughs. "Holy shit. You stole my wallet?"

"No!" I relax when I realize he's only kidding. "How did it get in here?"

He takes it from me, opens it, makes sure everything is still there. "I don't know."

"I must have taken it off the bar and put it with my stuff without realizing it." I cover my mouth with my hand. "I'm so sorry. I'm a total ditz. My head is always in the clouds."

"Hey. Don't worry about it." He takes my hand and pulls me to standing. Wraps his arms around me. "I'm just glad it was found."

I'm still totally embarrassed.

He reaches into the wallet and pulls something out, then throws it on the table next to me. "So I guess you'll have to forfeit your win on the hunt. Since you hid the winning item from me."

My eyes drift to the table. It's a license. A Texas license. With his name on it.

"Wait…" I look up at him. "You live in Hollywood."

He's grinning smugly. "I hate Hollywood. I grew up in San Antonio. My whole family's there. I never changed out my license because I always thought I'd go back. You can take the guy out of Texas but you can't take Texas out of the guy."

I smack him. "Why didn't you tell me?"

"Because you said you had to come all the way to New York for inspiration. I thought any girl who couldn't get inspired in her hometown had to have hated everything in it. Didn't want you hating me any more than you already did."

"I…that's not true. And I didn't hate you when I first met you. I just…"

Okay, yes I did. And yes, all I ever said to Lily, once Trevor dumped me, was how Austin was smothering me. The whole big state of Texas was smothering me, with its stupid men like Trevor who talked all sweet one day and then jumped into bed with someone else the next. I'd needed to escape, and so when Bryn had her crisis, I jumped.

But it's not the place. It's the person.

He puts a finger under my chin, raising my face up to his. "You said you didn't get a chance to research the city. What if I help you?"

I don't know. At this moment, I'm wondering why I set the book in New York to begin with. Before I thought it was so smart of me, to set it in a place where things happen, where billionaires grow on trees. Now…who even cares?

Well, I suppose it's too late to change the setting now.

I hesitate. "Do you know New York?"

"Hell, yeah. Well, not great. But I did live here for a year between high school and college. I know my way around." He lifts his wallet. "And now I have the required funds."

I nod. "Yes. Oh my god. *Yes.* That would be amazing."

"Good. Get your ass dressed. We're going out on the town."

So I do. I slip into a simple red sundress—the only remotely sexy thing I brought with me, and never had the chance to wear—and pile my wet hair atop my head.

He looks at me. "Fucking hell. You're gorgeous."

He doesn't look so bad himself. He's just wearing jeans, a t-shirt, and his beaten leather jacket, but…yummy. He holds the door open for me and as I pass by, I whisper, "I still won. You hid the shark's tooth from me, too."

He studies me, a superior look in his face. "Is that right?"

I nod. "But I'll let you have a wish, anyway."

chapter twenty-six

Noah

We take the elevator down to the lobby. I can't stop looking at the phenomenal woman next to me, in the little red dress. It's been ten years since I lived in Manhattan, so I can't fully trust myself not to get us completely lost, especially with her long, bare legs distracting me.

But fuck it, I'm going to give it a try. "Okay. So what do you want to know about New York?"

She shrugs. "Everything."

"What have you seen so far?" I ask, running through a mental list of sights she might want to see. It's a long list. Even with a few weeks, we'd miss a lot. "We don't have much time, and as your official tour guide, I want to make sure you get the most out of this."

"Um. Okay. Let's see. What have I seen already?" She thinks about this, and then starts listing them off on her hand. "The inside of my friend's apartment. The House of Sass

Warehouse downtown. I also saw Elmo humping a woman. Oh, and I got lost in Chelsea. So…anything but that?"

"You got lost in Chelsea?"

She nods.

"That's about where I used to live." We step through the revolving doors and I scratch my chin. "That's a tall order. You've seen so much. I hope I can top the…what did you say? Warehouse? And dammit. The Elmo-humping thing was first on my list."

She shrugs. "I know. No wonder my muse took a vacation."

The doorman asks if we need a cab and I shake my head. I'm still figuring out where to go. "All right. What you need to know about New York City. Well. It's a wonderful town. The Bronx is up." I point it out. "And the Batter—"

"Stop." She rolls her eyes at me. "Unless you're going to sing it."

I shove my hands in my pockets and clamp my mouth shut.

"What?" She pouts. "I really do want to hear you sing."

"I'm sorry. You've already used your wish," I say to her, checking the street signs, ignoring her pout. "So. You pretty much need to see everything. Minus Elmo. Let's narrow that down a little. What will help you write this book?"

"Well, I'd love to find the places Ben would frequent, like where he would live and eat and stuff like that."

I rub my jaw, thinking. "He's a billionaire?"

She nods.

"That's tough. When I lived in the Village, I lived in a studio apartment with five other guys," I tell her. "I think your

Ben would probably break out in hives if he ever went into my neighborhood."

"Well...that's still helpful, I guess. Leia is a recent college graduate trying to decide what to do with her life. But I mostly just based her on me and Bryn, so... I have her character pretty much down. I was really hoping I could learn more about the places he'd take her to sweep her off her feet."

"Okay, okay. Well. Romantic doesn't have to be expensive. Maybe your Ben is less pretentious? Despite whisking her off in his private jet to Paris on a moment's notice?"

She quirks an eyebrow at me. No, I will never let her live that down. "All right. But do you know the most romantic places in town?"

I nod. "I happen to know a few."

Another eyebrow raised. I wrap my arm around her waist and step her to the curb, narrowly avoiding a cyclist as I hail a cab. When one pulls to the curb, we climb inside. "Grand Banks," I tell the driver.

Her dress pulls up high on her thighs as she sits back. I avert my eyes so I'm not in danger of cutting this trip short and taking her right back to the hotel. This. Is. Important, I remind myself, though my cock has other ideas as to what ranks up there on the needs-to-happen list.

She reaches into her bag and pulls out a crumpled napkin and a pen. The napkin has writing all over it. She frowns as the cab slips out into a wall of traffic on 7th Ave.

She inhales. "What is that smell? I'm trying to put the essence of the city into words. The sights, the tastes, the smells..."

"To me, New York smells like coffee, chocolate, weed, some old lady's perfume, and garbage. All mixed together."

She sniffs some more, shrugs, writes it down. She looks fucking adorable there, writing down everything I say like an eager beaver. Cute Rebecca, with that pen in her hand. Sexy Rebecca, in that phenomenal dress. Everything Rebecca, all at once. She has absolutely no idea what she is doing to me.

As we nose through the Village, I point down Leroy Street. "I used to live in a place there. Above an Indian restaurant. We always smelled like curry."

She writes something else down on her napkin.

It takes about twenty more minutes to get downtown to the pier. When she steps out onto the curb, she shields her eyes from the setting sun and says, "What neighborhood is this?"

"Tribeca," I tell her. She's still busily writing stuff on her napkin that I have to hold her elbow. She'd probably trip over her own feet, she's so lost in her own thoughts.

"It's so nice," she murmurs, still scribbling. She's running out of napkin.

"Okay. Watch it. The pier is coming to an end." I wink at her, guiding her over the gangplank, onto the ship overlooking the harbor. "You don't get easily seasick, do you?"

She shakes her head, then whirls around at the sights—the Hudson, sparkling in the setting sun, the skyline of Jersey City in the distance. "Oh my gosh. There's the Freedom Tower. Oh! And there's the Statue of Liberty!"

I nod. "Thought you might want to eat outside. I know it's a little cold, but—"

She bobs her head excitedly as we walk to the bar. "This is perfect."

"Food's okay. But I thought you'd get the most out of the view. Especially at sunset."

We sit at a table at the bow of the old wooden ship, and I give her the view facing the setting sun, so she can record it all. It's orange and pink and the clouds look like cotton candy—we couldn't have ordered a more perfect sunset. I give her my jacket to wear because it's kind of cold. We order champagne, caviar, and lobster rolls, since she's never had any of it and seems convinced Ben would.

I keep feeding her napkins to write on. She fills at least five of them up, stuffing them into her purse. The breeze is stiff and the boat a little rocky, so I keep watch to make sure she doesn't forget herself and let a napkin go flying into the Hudson.

"Thank you," she says to me as she sighs at the sight of the sunset. "This is going to make a great spot for their first date."

"I thought that their first kiss was in front of the Eiffel Tower," I say.

She lets out a dreamy sigh and her head drops onto my shoulder. "I might change it."

I take a napkin from her and tuck it safely into her purse, then duck down so my lips are near her ear. I kiss the shell of it and smile. "It's not over. You've still got a lot of pages to fill, Rebecca."

chapter twenty-seven

Becka

This is amazing.

After we watch the sunset, we make our way on something called the Hudson River Greenway to the Freedom Tower, where we take super-fast elevators up to the One World Observatory and Noah shows me sights from a distance as we sip—what else?—Manhattans. Then we walk to the 9/11 Memorial, and stop at a wine bar for a glass of pinot grigio. The bottle of champagne at dinner had me a little tipsy, but the Manhattan and the glass of wine have me in danger of not remembering any of this night.

Thank god for my napkins. Even though I'm not sure I'll be able to read any of them when I get home. I really do need a better system for keeping my notes.

At shortly after ten, we're sitting in the wine bar, and I'm trying to copy my notes more legibly onto another napkin. He's watching me carefully transcribing each word. "I wish we could've seen more," he says.

"No. This was unforgettable. I saw so much more in four hours than I did the whole week I was here. Really."

"Which is why you have to write it all down?"

I ignore the joke, read my notes, and frown. "I still just don't know what to do after the black moment."

He takes a gulp of wine and frowns. "Black moment. That sounds contagious."

I grin at him. As hot as he is, sometimes he can be helplessly adorable. "The black moment in a book is when everything looks doomed to failure. So Ben is set to take over his father's position as CEO of the largest corporation in New York, and Leia is following her dream of becoming a marine biologist and was just offered a job in Florida. Neither one of them is willing to budge, because of their careers. And they shouldn't have to, you know? So, doom and gloom."

"Yeah. Got it."

"Now what? Now, it all works out, and Happily Ever After. Or it should. But it just isn't." I frown into my glass. "It just doesn't make sense. I created this whole drama about them not being together. But they're supposed to be super in love. I mean, it's not believable that they somehow cannot make it work."

"Why not? I mean, I want a serious role, but it's not easy to get it. You want to finish this book, but you're still struggling to figure out how yet." He shrugs. "In real life, things don't just work out in a blink. People spend most of their lives in flux. Knowing what would make them happy, but saying 'Some day' instead of 'Right now' because obligations or geography or their own fears keep them from what they really want."

"I guess. But I can't just end it with them saying, 'Some day.' Ben has to sacrifice a lot to be with her—or she does."

"Or they compromise," he suggests.

"But how?"

He thinks. "You're calling the shots. Anything could happen."

"Like what?"

He presses his lips together, concentrating really hard, so by the time his eyes light with an idea, I think it must be the answer to all of my problems. "Like, maybe aliens attack and destroy New York? And then they have to fight for sur—"

"Stop," I moan. "It's a romance."

"And who's saying you can't have sex during the apocalypse?"

I frown at him. "You are officially flagged from ever giving me plot ideas."

"All right, all right. But the way I see it, what you need is a reason for them to make their Some Day be Right Now. That's all."

That makes sense. I sit there, nursing my wine and thinking as he pays the check. What would make them both or either of them willing to drop everything they worked for to just be together? If either of them sacrifice their career, won't they end up regretting it in the end?

Ugh. This is painful.

He pays the check, and I gather up my small pile of napkins. We leave the café. The second we walk out, a guy bumps into me.

"Hey. Watch it." Noah's hand flashes out to pull me to his side, and he shoots the guy a glare before he scurries off. "There's New York for you." He smiles down at me, and for a minute I can only look at that smile and wonder if the next time I'll see it, it'll be through a movie screen.

The thought depresses me so much I instantly look away.

"So." He claps his hands and rubs them. "Back to business. Ben. That fucking asshole doesn't deserve your girl Leia. But that's beside the point because he's what she wants."

"Ben is not an asshole!" Well. Not that much, anyway. "He's alpha. It's what women want."

"A guy who treats you like shit, then makes it all better with a fuck, is that what every woman wants?"

"No! He…" I scowl. "It's a fantasy. You get to experience a guy who is rough around the edges change his ways because of his deep love for a woman."

"Right. He was wounded emotionally as a child." He frowns thoughtfully. "How deeply can you change? For how long?"

"For forever!" I groan. "The woman's love transforms him. You don't get it. I mean, how can you? Have you ever even been in a relationship?"

"No." He eyes me. "Relationships aren't exactly the strong suit of Hollywood. You?"

"I…" I think of Trevor. "I was dating this guy. Then he cheated and that was the end of it."

"On you? Bastard. Was it a long-term thing?"

I blow out a huff of air. "No. That's the embarrassing thing. We were only dating three weeks. Which was, incidentally, the longest relationship I'd ever had."

"Ah."

"Which is probably why I make up romances instead of living them. Real-life romance is way too complicated." And now I'm blushing. I've said too much. "But I don't really want to talk about that."

He seems so genuinely shocked and perturbed by what I just said that I reach out to run my thumb along his lips. His sexy, wicked mouth.

"I'd never cheat on you." His voice is low and gruff, as if he's just made a confession. And he sounds so honest, my heart skips a beat.

I let myself wonder about what it would be like to date him. To be with him, as a couple. Would he move to Austin? Would I move to Hollywood? It sounds so impossible my stomach is in knots by the mere realization that Noah can't be my forever. No matter how deliciously he fucks. How much he's…well, gotten under my skin. Under my skin? He's in my veins, the fucker.

It's already a concern to imagine how hard it'll be to get him out of there. I mean, geez, Trevor was three weeks of nothing, and when he betrayed me, it sent me into a tailspin. I don't want Noah to be the new Trevor. If he is, it'll be a million times worse. I might never recover.

"How do you know you wouldn't cheat? You just said you've never been in a relationship."

He shoves his hands deep into his pockets and hitches a shoulder, making the sandy hair tumble over his forehead. "I just wouldn't. I've had flings, Rebecca. I would know when I have something special and I'd hold it close and never let go."

I stare at him, going weak in the knees.

I want to ask him what will happen tomorrow, when we have to go our separate ways.

But I don't want to.

Walking hand in hand with him, in this city I once hated, right now…it's perfect.

And I don't want to ruin it with talk of goodbyes.

chapter twenty-eight

Noah

After the café, we take a cab up to the Theater District, where we check out the different plays. I show her where my crappy Hamlet audition was, and the Broadhurst Theater, where I spent that year in *Les Mis* before it finally closed down.

She's so excited by all of it, utterly star struck. "I think," she says as I lead her into a little gift shop, "that I might have been too hasty with bashing those superhero movies. Maybe I should give them another try. Everyone likes them so much."

I shake my head. "Your initial impression is right on the money. Believe me. But yeah. Membership in the Superhero Club has its privileges. I almost got arrested for stealing your laptop. Megalith got me out of that one."

The store is crowded. We're walking among racks of I Love NY tchotchkes, postcards, t-shirts, bumper stickers, magnets, and shot glasses. She lifts one up and sets it down, raising an eyebrow at me. "Seriously?"

I nod. "Turns out airport security guards were big fans. Also…your initial impression about stalker professor man was right on the money."

She takes a postcard of the arch at Washington Square from a display, reads the caption, and then sets it back in the wire rack. "Wait. What do you mean? You mean that guy with the creepy stare and the tweed blazer?"

I nod. "I mean that he was the one who stole your laptop."

Something dawns on her face, lighting up as she tries to put a shot glass back and misses. It tumbles over but she catches it in time. "Oh, my god. That's why he looked so familiar. He was sitting at the original gate with me. I'd been typing away on my book, oblivious as usual. Of course! How did you catch him?"

I yawn. It feels like a lifetime ago. "I saw it in his bag and I caught up with him, and he tried to blame me. It was a cluster fuck. Eventually it all got sorted out. But if it wasn't for Megalith, I'd probably be in prison right now. The security guards love Galaxy Titans."

She brings her hand to her mouth. "See. You are a hero. My hero, at least. And you know what? You might hate being Megalith, but you make a lot of people happy as him. I bet a lot of kids look up to you."

She looks up at me with a hopeful expression. I brush the hair out of her face, duck down and graze my lips over hers, tasting the sweetness of the wine on her lips. I instantly want more. If anything can make Broadway the street of my dreams again, it's her. Being Megalith doesn't suck nearly as much, with her.

Oh, shit.

Megalith.

I forgot. I'm supposed to be in the make-up chair tomorrow at six a.m.

I tell her I need a minute to make a call, then look for an out-of-the-way place, but the shop is full. I lose her among the souvenirs and when I find her next, she's holding a small pile of things. A t-shirt, a pen, a few postcards. "I didn't want to remember New York before," she confesses, her cheeks pink. "But now I kind of do."

I take them from her. "Allow me."

"Oh, I can't let you—"

I hold up a hand to her. "It's my pleasure."

I find a few other things, then walk up to the cash register, dialing Anne as I go. When she answers, I say, "Hey."

A pause. "You're not on a plane. And that worries me."

"Yeah, look." I push Rebecca's souvenirs onto the counter and the cashier begins to ring them up. "I know you've already moved the *King of the Galaxy* shoot for me, but can we possibly move them one more time? I promise. This is the last time I'll ask."

Her tone is hard. "Why? What happened?"

I push my credit card toward the cashier. "Talk to airport security at JFK. They retained me on suspected theft, long enough that when I got to the gate, the plane was leaving. My only saving grace was Megalith."

It's the truth. Even though I'm not sure I would've made the flight, anyway.

Anne sighs. "Oh. So that's why you're all over Twitter. Seems a lot of people have pictures with you."

"I told you it's the truth," I say as the cashier, a young African American, lifts my credit card, and looks at me.

"By the way, you should really be tweeting more," she tells me. "It'll—"

"I know, I know," I mutter. It's an ongoing war between Anne and me. Strangely enough, I have hundreds of thousands of followers who don't seem to care that I've tweeted maybe ten times in my life. I just can't get into the social media shit.

"Wait... *King of the Galaxy?*" the cashier exclaims. "Are you... Megalith? You're Megalith? Holy shit!"

He starts scanning the store for someone, anyone to tell.

I nod at the man, who motions to another clerk. Now they're both gawking at me. "Yeah. Okay. So I'll be in tomorrow night. Got to go."

"All right. I'll call them right now and explain. But I get the feeling you might be off the movie pos—"

Ah, fuck the movie posters. I hang up as the female clerk reaches into her apron and pulls out her phone. "Can I get a selfie with you?"

I nod and lean over the counter so she can take one.

People in New York, like those in Hollywood, are pretty chill when it comes to meeting actors. They see them all the time, so it's not a big deal. Unfortunately, I'm in a gift shop, where pretty much all of the clientele are tourists.

The phrase "flies on shit" comes to mind.

Now every person in the busy store is starting to catch on. It's about to get bad. I've never been overwhelmed before, but I've seen it happen to other actors. It can cause a pandemonium. Any more of this, and I might not be able to escape.

The cashier jumps over the counter with my bag, camera at the ready. He snaps a picture of the two of us and then hands me my loot. "Really cool to meet you, Steele. Hope you nail

Buzzkill in the next movie. Fucking sucks what he did to your best friend."

The girl nods. "I cried for you. You're so strong."

It kills me when people really think I'm Megalith. They think a blue guy who crushes mountains is an actual person, and despite looking nothing like him, I'm still him. This happens to me often at Comic-Con, where people can be quite fanatical about me. They know things about the character of Megalith that even I don't know.

"Thanks. Good to meet you." I start to move toward the exit, as I'm approached by three teenagers and their mother. They want my picture, as well.

I glance over the sea of heads, now tightly assembling around me, leaving no escape. Rebecca is standing in a corner, watching, an astonished look on her face, as now people start pouring in through the entrance. I can't tell if she's worried or not, until she meets my gaze and smiles with a look like, *Does this happen often*?

A half hour later, I finally break free of the crowd and get to Rebecca. I hold up her bag for her. "Sorry for the delay. The perils of being a star." I do jazz hands to show her I use the word loosely.

"No, it's okay..." She laughs. "I just feel stupid because it took me so long to know who you were. People love you."

"Most people don't usually recognize me unless I'm in make-up or someone points me out..." I shove my hands into the pockets of my jeans as we step out onto the dark city street. It feels good to have air in my lungs again.

"You don't care?"

"I do. But I'm here, in this city, for one reason only. And it's not because of the blue asshole. It's because of you. It's not even because of the sights. The only sight I want to see right now is *you*. Preferably naked. On top of me."

She stops and looks up at me, licking her lips. "How far are we from the hotel?"

My eyes don't leave hers. "Five minutes, by cab."

A slow smile spreads over her face. "Then let's do that."

She doesn't have to ask me twice. I'm at the curb, hailing the cab, as soon as the words leave her mouth. Then I take her hand, tight, in mine, and slide in beside her.

chapter twenty-nine

Becka

The ride back to the hotel might be only six minutes, but he makes the most of it. The second we get into the car he brings his hand to my jaw. He ducks his mouth down and kisses me, his eyes darkening. “Good plan,” he murmurs. “I approve.”

“The city’s nice, but to tell you the truth,” I whisper as his hand moves down, molding my breast, making the nipple harden at once, “I haven’t seen anything better than what I saw in that hotel room.”

His fingers graze the edge of the halter, near my collarbone, as his eyes take me in. My nipples are hard, practically begging for him. The streetlights outside flash across his face, illuminating the hungry look in his eyes. “Does Ben know how lucky he is?”

He trails his tongue down my neck, and his hand reaches for the hem of my skirt, gradually working his way between my thighs. When he reaches the sensitive place where they meet, his fingers lightly graze my clit, and I let out a groan from deep inside.

His eyes widen as he realizes I'm not wearing panties.

"Research," I breathe out as his thumb finds the sensitive nub. I arch my back.

He takes my earlobe into his mouth. His other hand flirts with the tie of my halter dress at my neck. His voice is ragged. "So if I pull on this string, what will happen?"

"You can find out," I tease.

"Interesting." He doesn't pull, though. He's saving that, his fingers lightly playing with the skin at the nape of my neck while his breath is hot on my skin. His hand moves over my mound, harder now. "What would Ben do now?"

I close my eyes. Ben would always do the right thing. But Noah clearly doesn't need any help in knowing what that is. "He'd do that," I rasp out.

I spread my legs apart, and he slowly inserts a finger into me. I moan.

"I can't wait to be here. In you. I've been thinking about it since we left."

We arrive at the hotel and it's all a blur, taking the elevator up to the giant penthouse hotel room. When we get inside, I drop my purse and he drops the package in the entryway, and he pulls me flush against him.

"So," he says, his finger leisurely grazing my lips as his eyes fall on me. "I'm interested in understanding your characters. Tell me more."

I smile, skirt away from him, taking his hand and leading him closer to the bed. "Like?"

I whirl to him and breath and sane thought escapes me. He bridges the distance in one sure step, and my body ripples with anticipation. I place both my hands on his hard chest. I feel the wild beat of his heart under the thin fabric of the t-shirt, a stuttering rhythm that matches my own.

"Like…" He reaches out, and slowly circles my nipple through the fabric with the pad of his thumb, making it stiffen, then walks his finger up to the string at my neck. "Would Ben fuck her slow?"

The intensity in his eyes levels me. My knees wobble. "Yes."

He finally pulls the string, and the fabric gapes at once, tumbling down over my breasts. With one quick movement, he wraps his arms around my ass and boosts me up into his arms. My thighs settle on his hips as he pulls my skirt up to my waist.

"Would he be gentle, Rebecca?" he husks out, pressing his erection into my bare core, anything but gently.

"Yes…well…" I hesitate, lost in sensation. Ben *would* be gentle. But that doesn't mean that's what I want right now. "Ah, yes," I then say.

He devours my lips, walking us to the window. He removes one hand from cradling my back and rips aside the blackout curtain. He slams me against the window, completely commanding me with his mouth, body, hands.

"No. *No*, Texas. He'd fuck her fast and hard because he wants her that much."

Yes. *Yes*. Fuck Ben. *That's* what I want.

Noah stops for a moment and I hear the movement of hardware behind us. I clutch eagerly to him, my body overcome by hunger, wanting anything but to stop. Then he slips open a sliding door and I feel a breeze embrace my back. He walks me out into the darkness and settles me down onto a pillowed sofa…a lounge. I look up, and all I can see above us are the stars.

I gasp, reaching up to grab for his t-shirt. "I want to see you."

"That Leia talking?"

"No. That's me," I growl possessively, pulling his t-shirt over his head so my hands can roam over his taut muscles, the smooth planes of his perfect body. I run my fingernails down his back and under the waistband of his jeans, gripping his hard ass. "Fuck me fast. Hard."

He opens his jeans, shoving them down over his hips, and positions himself between my trembling thighs. And then he pushes inside me, hard, owning my body. He lets out a tormented groan, covering me in his body and we tangle together in a madness of hot, greedy kisses.

I move with his movements, lost in the waves of sensation pulsing through me. He lifts me from the lounge, drilling into me, fucking me harder than ever before. I growl. "Oh god, Noah."

"You like it fast? Hard?" he grinds out as I feel him starting to come apart. He angles deeper, and I cry out, every thrust sending me closer and closer to that edge. He's gasping and growling and so fucking feral and wild, his body slamming into mine, and all I can think is that slow and tender and stars overhead is so overrated, and Ben *is* a total asshole.

Because no. God, no. It's not even close to what my hero would do.

It's so much better than any writer could ever put into words.

chapter thirty

Noah

I don't want to fall asleep. If I do, when we wake up, we'll only have a short time before we have to return to the real world.

And I'm not sure I want to go yet.

So we don't sleep. It's after one, might even be two, but I don't want to check my phone to see.

I don't want to know.

I help her sort out her napkins, and she turns them over, reading them, squinting, trying to make heads or tails of them so she can transcribe them into her laptop. When she shakes her head hopelessly, I throw the bag from the gift shop at her.

She shoots me a confused look.

"Did you even look inside?" I ask.

She noses open the bag and pulls it out. It's a fancy leather-bound journal, tied with a strap, with the words embossed on the front: *Either write something worth reading or do something worth writing—Ben Franklin*

She looks up at me. "You got this for me? When?"

"When I was checking out. It seemed appropriate. We can't have your napkins blowing all over the city."

She clasps her hands together, then leans over and kisses me. "Oh, gosh. It's perfect. Thank you so much."

She starts transcribing the napkins onto her new journal. I find *Revenge of The Galaxy,* Galaxy Titans Volume Two, on TBS, and we watch it, even though she has no idea what's going on. I try to explain things as best I can, but she's clearly lost. Still, she gets excited every time I'm on the screen.

"It's not *Going Home,* but you're really good," she says, snuggling next to me on the bed, her hot naked body pressed against my side. "And I think you're wrong. I really don't think anyone else could play him. You lend a certain humanity to him."

I study the screen. In the scene, I'm crushing the Golden Gate Bridge to keep BuzzKill from bombing San Francisco. "You think?"

"Yeah. I do. It's not easy to love a stone man. But all those people in the gift shop today…they love you. Not just Megalith. You *as* Megalith." She smiles. "And they'll love you in other roles, too. You just have to find the right ones. Get lucky."

Yeah. I need to remove the chip off my shoulder. Adopt a new attitude. It sounds easy. But will my head get in the way? I guess I won't know unless I try.

And I'm ready to try.

"I'll show you getting lucky," I say, taking her wrists and rolling on top of her. "By the way, I'm getting you a Cronut tomorrow for breakfast."

She wrinkles her nose. "A cross between a croissant and a donut?"

I nod. "Not a fan? They were invented in a place downtown. You have to have an original Cronut. I once waited in line for six hours for one. It's my new mission for you."

"If you insist."

"I do." I kiss her lightly, just grazing her lips. "Then you might be able to consider your first trip to New York a success."

She pushes on my chest. "I already do. I feel… I don't know. Inspired."

She's right. I had enough shit happen to me during this trip, but would I do it over again? Hell yes.

Tomorrow, it's over. Today, actually. We always knew that this would end. We'll take the plane and I'll leave her at her gate and chalk this up to a good memory, nothing more. That's what needs to happen. That's the natural way of things. This was just a pause in our normal lives. A vacation. Soon, we'll be back to business.

I've been putting it off long enough. I have to get back to Megalith. More than ever, I know it's what I need to do.

Then why is it so damn hard?

chapter thirty-one

Becka

We wake up early. When the sun is just making its way over the horizon, striping orange rays and the shadows from buildings through the windows, I feel him stir next to me, a hand roaming possessively over me to drag me to him. I feel his erection, his hard body, pressing into mine as he presses a kiss into my temple.

I roll over onto my elbow and look at him. His eyes are open, like he's been awake for hours.

We stay quiet. For like an hour, just quiet, the only sound the occasional running of water from hotel rooms nearby.

We're getting ready to go. Mentally, that is. Because physically, we're still in bed. I'm on my side facing him. He's on his side, facing me. His hand is roving up and down my arm, alighting goosebumps everywhere. But his eyes don't move from mine.

My mind should be on what I need to pack so I don't forget or lose something. Making sure we check out and get a cab in plenty of time to make it through security. But no. My thoughts are caught on leaving this bed. My skin separating from his. His gaze loosening on mine, never staring at me with such intensity again.

What if I never feel this way, for the rest of my life?

When he speaks, his voice is gentle. “So. Ready to go back home?”

No, I want to answer. I can’t even force out a yes because he’s staring at me so intently. I manage a smile. “I guess. You?”

He yawns. “Ready as I’ll ever be. Not looking forward to facing that hellhole again.”

This is where we should roll out, get our asses moving. Climb into the shower. Start that dreaded morning routine that has never felt quite so dreadful until this very moment.

One corner of his mouth quirks up. “One more for the road?”

My entire body heats up at the prospect. Noah’s ashy-gray eyes have never looked so dark before.

“Unless,” he adds quietly, “you insist on that Mile High Club thing, but I’ll have to insist that a bed is far, far better.”

I reach out and grab the back of his hair, easing closer to set my mouth on his. He groans softly and shifts so he can smother my mouth with his, and run one of his hands up and down my side.

We’re kissing leisurely, slow but so deep, my toes are curling right where they’re tangled with the sheets. Noah kicks them completely off of us and shifts above me. His erection digs into my tummy. I like it. Love it. I love the way his hand keeps moving up my side, only to still in my hair, and hold me still for his onslaught.

I love how we don't say anything else as I part my legs a little wider, so that his hips can sink between my thighs. And his cock pulses at my wettest, hottest spot. I love that we groan together at the same time that he drives in me. Love the way he clutches my hands over my head all of a sudden. Holds my gaze like he can't take his eyes away from my own. Love the way his shark tooth dances on the nook at the bottom of his thick throat as he moves. The way his chest rises and falls faster, a little more unevenly. The way he smells the same as I do—like the hotel room shampoo and conditioner and soap we both washed with—but at the same time he smells different. Like him.

I love how the sunlight coming up outside the window seems to greet our entwined bodies with a thousand and one tiny kisses. I love how New York is suddenly the best place on earth. I love that I'm alive right at this moment, in this city, with this guy, in this very room, and suddenly I love every coincidence and event that happened in my life to lead me here.

I love…

Brock.

And Megalith.

And more than anything I love Noah Steele.

And as that shocking, soul-crushing, heart-rending realization hits me, I'm hit with the excruciatingly delicious feeling of exploding into a thousand pieces for him. And while I know I can recover from this explosion in a few minutes, I know that when we say goodbye, there are pieces of me he will take that I will never recover.

The more I keep pretending that this can lead somewhere, the less chance I'll be able to finish Ben and Leia's story. The less chance I'll be able to write anything good, ever again.

I have to protect myself. Get out of this while I still can, before I cause irreversible damage and I can never climb out of this hole.

When I come, I bury my face in his shoulder so he won't see the tears.

chapter thirty-two

Noah

Stepping out of the room that morning with our bags feels like hell.

It's like the first tiny tear in a hole that's going to grow wider and wider as the day goes on. In the end, in Dallas, we'll be separated for good.

This shouldn't matter to me. I've lived in Hollywood long enough that I thought I had the Hollywood lifestyle down. You love. You leave. You play it loose. The end. I've had plenty of one-night stands that could've been more, but weren't worth the effort.

But Hollywood is plastic. Fake. And she's the realest thing I've ever known. I can't help thinking that I still got a lot more Texas in me. That this is something I need to hold onto.

We take the elevator to the lobby, and she's staring at the numbers, a look of concentration on her face. She seems more closed-off suddenly, ever since we started getting ready to leave, like she's preparing for the inevitable.

I reach my finger out and try to smooth out the crease of worry between her eyes. She's quiet. She might be thinking of leaving. How she doesn't want to.

The chasm of unsaid things between us widens further.

Soon it will be too late to say any of them at all.

But we still have a couple of good hours of exploring the city left. I'm not going to ruin this moment by doing that.

We get into a cab and I hold her hand. I ask the driver to take us past a few places we've missed. Rockefeller Center. The Empire State Building. The Arch at Washington Square Park. Then we go to Dominique Ansel's bakery in SoHo, where we wait in a block-long line for about ten minutes before we're told that they've sold out.

"Well, fuck," I say as the crowd dissipates around us. "Should have come here, first."

She hitches a shoulder. "It's okay. I don't really like donuts. Or croissants for that matter."

"Yes, but how often are you in New York?"

"Never. Bryn doesn't need me anymore, and it's not like I have the money in my bank account to jet-set everywhere." She sighs. "I suspect that this is a once in a life-time trip."

"Right. So I feel bad. You didn't get a big enough taste of the Big Apple. That's a problem. I think it means we must meet again so I can show you the rest. My treat."

I wait for her to bite. But she doesn't.

"Well, the next best thing I can get you is a pretzel," I tell her, pointing out the nearest pretzel cart.

"I like pretzels," she says.

I get one to share, give her the bigger part. We wander up and down the streets, talking and eating, heading north toward Broadway, because somehow my mind is always trained on that part of the city. "So, where do you live in Austin?" I ask her.

"South of the city," she says. "By the track."

"Yeah? My aunt lives up there. In Elroy? She used to run a daycare there."

"Which one?"

"Safe and Sound, I think."

Rebecca pops a ragged piece of pretzel into her mouth and her eyes widen. "Is your Aunt named Lydia?"

I nod.

"Holy…she was my babysitter. She practically raised me while my parents were working."

"Hell. Small world," I say, polishing off the pretzel and tossing the wax paper in the trash.

"Small? This is almost creepy! Don't you think?"

Not creepy. Meant to be. Like all this shit is pointing in a definite direction, and I just need to stop moaning about what life hasn't given me and let fate take the wheel for once.

It all but assures me that we can't end things. Not now. Not with everything that destiny has done trying to throw our asses together.

I open my mouth to tell her that.

But as I do, I realize she's frowning, her mind more on the creepiness of that coincidence than on the fact that it's a sign we need to somehow continue this. When I start to ask her what's wrong, she stops short, her eyes trained on something across the street.

"Oh, my gosh. I know her," she says, nudging me as I spot a tall, lithe girl with a bun and a duffel bag walking along the sidewalk. "That's Sara. My best friend's roommate."

"Yeah?" Something inside me constricts. It's got to be after ten by now. We need to hail that cab. And all my chances to get this out will be gone.

I do not need this fucking interference. Not now.

She's already crossing the side street to her, waving, but I hang back.

"Come on," she says, motioning me to follow her. "She's auditioning for Broadway, too. I bet that's why she's here so early. I bet you'd have a lot to talk about."

The last thing I need is to meet her friends. I can't even pretend to be charming right now. I shake my head, then shove my hands deep into the pockets of my jeans. "You go ahead."

I watch her go over to Sara and start talking animatedly. Meanwhile, I lean against a lamppost, counting the seconds ticking away. One, one thousand, two, one thousand. Mid-conversation, her friend turns away and starts talking to a guy in a suit, with a dog, and I lose count of the seconds. Something hot and dangerous pulses through my veins.

Because that's Ben.

Rebecca's Ben.

But she barely glances his way. There he is, her ideal man, and she doesn't even look twice. And he's not looking at her. It's clear there's zero love connection and he's only interested in Sara. When Sara calls her over, she shakes his hand stiffly, formally.

I go back to counting the seconds. A moment later she calls a goodbye and heads over to me, all smiles, breathless. "All these weird coincidences! I was staying in her apartment while I was here. In Nolita?" She stops when she reaches me, concerned. "Everything okay?"

I hold up my phone. "We'd better get to the airport."

She presses her lips together. "All right."

Is it? Because as I hail a cab and we climb inside, nothing about this seems all right.

So I take a breath. And I jump.

"What if we arrange to meet again?" I venture as she piles her carry-on onto her lap and lets out a sigh.

She turns to look at me, eyes wide. "What?"

"I know, I know. We said we wouldn't."

She's shaking her head. "I have about two months left to finish this book before my parents stop helping me with rent on my apartment. And you have to get back to Hollywood. We can't."

"I know. We've both got to get our careers in line right now. That's a big thing. But what if we meet…" I scratch at my chin. "In six months. Actually, April 12. For the premiere of *King of the Galaxy.* You'd come to that, right?"

But she's just staring at her knees.

I thought the crease would disappear. It doesn't. It widens.

Something inside me tightens. So that wasn't what she was thinking.

Finally, I give up. "So that's a no?"

She inhales deeply. "I'm thinking of movies. Like *An Affair to Remember. Serendipity. Before Sunrise*. Have you seen any of those?"

It's not what I expected. "Yeah. I guess."

"Well, in all of those, there's a guy, and a girl. And when they separate…they agree to meet at a certain place, at a certain time, in the future." She's gnawing on her lip.

"Wait. *An Affair to Remember*? That's the one with the Empire State Building, right? And *Before Sunrise*...that had sequels?"

She nods. But that doesn't explain why she looks so worried.

"And?"

She slumps in her seat. "And it doesn't work out. Life gets in the way, and they all end up missing their connection."

"Okay…so?"

"So let's not do that, all right? Let's not fool ourselves and say we're going to meet somewhere, later. Because you and I know it won't happen." She sighs. "I don't want to get my hopes up."

"It *could* happen," I point out.

She shakes her head. "No," she mumbles. "I'm not that lucky. And once in a lifetime doesn't happen twice."

chapter thirty-three

Becka

We're mostly silent as we go through the security line.

I think he's upset at me. And I guess I would be, too. He made the overture to see me again, and I turned him down.

I must be insane.

But it makes sense. I can't and will not spend the next six months hoping and dreaming and waiting to see him again, when we know we both live totally different lives. He's in Hollywood, for god's sake, land of the beautiful. Women probably throw themselves at him once a day there. And in six months, that'll be...what? One hundred and eighty women? One hundred and eighty chances to forget about me?

No.

This is a happy ending on its own. We had a great time. But some things are just better when they end. We don't need a sequel, because sequels never live up to the original.

I filled my notebook with ideas. Now I need to get home and concentrate on figuring out an ending for my book before my parents cut me off for good.

We got our bags from the hotel, and got to the gate plenty early. Noah goes off to Hudson News for something. He doesn't say as much, but I think it's because he's disappointed in me. But he'll get over it. He's never been in a real relationship, probably because he's not capable of one. He's the big Hollywood movie star, and they don't really do healthy relationships.

I'm nobody. And if Trevor's any indication, I fall way too hard. I need to steel myself.

As I wait, I look at my phone. I was able to charge it fully at the hotel. Last night, I'd found a half-dozen messages from Lily, each one more worried than the previous:

Lily: ***Back from the bar. How's your hunk of stone?***

Lily: ***Hello?***

Lily: ***I'm hoping Megalith didn't kidnap you and take you to his lair.***

Lily: ***???***

Lily: ***WHY AREN'T YOU ANSWERING ME????***

The last one was sent just an hour ago:

Lily: ***Becka. This is serious. Where the hell are you?***

Me: ***I'm here. Sorry. Still at JFK. Missed the flight again.***

Lily: ***Did Megalith have anything to do with it?***

Me: ***He had EVERYTHING to do with it…but it's over. Coming home now.***

Lily: ***Are you kidding me? Do you have his phone number? You can call him, right? You can't just END IT. Can you?***

Me: ***I can. I will.***

I frown at my phone. I can. I can I can I can.

And yes, I have his number. But not for long.

I open up my contacts list, find his number, my finger hovering over the Delete Contact button.

Then I do it. Gone. Just as easily as he'll be gone from my life.

The black hole in my stomach starts to open at once. It's gnawing, growing, eating away at my insides.

I shift in my seat, certain it would only be worse six months from now. Or one month from now, when I open up the TMZ website to see gossip about which Hollywood starlet he's frolicking with. He can easily wipe me from his memory. For me…it's going to be impossible.

Good. I'm glad I deleted his number. I don't think I'm above drunk texting him at three in the morning.

That smug satisfaction with myself lasts only until he returns, two bottles of Aquafina in his hands. He hands one to me and slumps into the seat beside me. "You okay?" he asks.

I nod. That gnawing feeling is anything *but* okay, though.

We only have twenty minutes before boarding. I pull out my laptop and try to get to work, adding setting details to my novel. But I can't. Either Bitch Muse isn't cooperating again, or she's intent that I not waste these last moments with Noah.

I know I'm wasting them. Soon we'll be on the plane and we'll be apart from one another. This is terrible. Sad and terrible and I know that I am not meant for one-night-stands. Or two-night-stands. Or whatever the hell we had.

I can't. I'm frozen. Afraid of adding more to the list of things I love about Noah Steele, a list that's getting ready to topple all over me.

A moment later, he says to me, "Hey. What seat do you have?"

I reach for my phone and pull up my ticket. I wince. The airport gods clearly hate me. "Ugh. 34E. Again?"

He grins. "Best seat on the plane."

"I thought you said…" I start, trailing off when he holds his phone with his mobile pass out to me.

34F. He's sitting right next to me.

So we'll have another three hours together.

Prolonging our inevitable goodbye. Still, my heart leaps before my head fully processes it.

But is it inevitable? I could take a risk. I mean, all love is about taking risk. As impossible as we are, even if there's one chance in a million this could work…maybe it's worth it.

I look up at him, and his eyes are hooded and cautious.

Lily would approve. Bryn would be my cheerleader. They would wholeheartedly approve of me going for this.

So I should. I should just pour it out, let things happen, and take that leap.

"Um…" I start.

"I got it," he says, glancing away. As if he's afraid of settling too hard on me because he knows I'm not going to last. "I'll trade seats with you, if you want."

It nearly tears a whimper from my throat. No, that wasn't it.

But I nod, power down my computer, and swallow all the unspoken words inside me. I close the lid on my laptop, shove it into my bag, and pull out my unread copy of *Glamour*. "Thank you. That's very kind of you."

chapter thirty-four

Noah

Something has shifted again by the time we board the flight. As I suspected, we're in the last row of the plane. When she moves in, plops in her seat and I sit beside her, she stuffs her carry-on under the seat and places her magazine in the front pocket, then dips her head to peer out the oval window. Her face is flushed.

It's stuffy in here, so I twist the vent to let the air come in. "Better?"

She slips her seatbelt over her lap and white-knuckles the armrests.

"You don't like flying, do you?"

She swallows. "I don't know."

I lean back, pry her fingers off the plastic armrest between us, then twine my fingers with hers. "Just a feeling. How did you make it here?"

"It was better before you. I don't know what's wrong with me."

Her eyes drift over our clasped hands. Her brow is sheened with sweat and she has a helpless look on her face. Like she might bolt from the plane.

I think of the first time I met her. When she was doubled over at the first gate, looking much the same. I debate whether I should reach for the paper bag in the seat back. "You have panic attacks?"

She nods.

"I've got you," I tell her in a soothing voice. "Don't worry."

I reach over and close the window shade so it's just the two of us. No one sits beside us as the flight attendant announces that all passengers have boarded and that the doors are being closed. She's breathing heavy, like she had been that first time I met her, and her eyes are clouding over. This isn't good.

"Do you want me to give you space?" I ask her, still holding her hand. "I can move—"

"No!" she says. "I like you right there."

I offer her a stick of chewing gum, but she swats it away. I open the top of her water and hand it to her. "Drink this?"

She shakes her head, pushing me off as the plane starts to wheel away from the terminal. "I'm good. I'll be fine once the plane takes off."

"Okay."

I watch her carefully, eyes closed, chest heaving as the plane makes its way to the runway, stopping and starting over the next few minutes. That crease of worry between her eyes doesn't go away. When we wheel out onto the runway and the plane starts to pick up speed, she squeezes my hand.

And we're off.

I wait as we rise higher and higher into the sky. For her to loosen her grip. To let go. To tell me she's ready. But she doesn't. Her breathing comes faster.

"Noah," she says, opening her eyes. "I can't do this."

"Yes, you can," I tell her.

She looks around, eyes wild. Her voice is louder now. "No."

She lurches forward, trying to stand. The seatbelt holds her back. She drops my hand and scrabbles for it. "What are you… Rebecca," I say calmly. "You can't."

People in seats around us are noticing now. The flight attendant comes past and notices her. "Seatbelts on, please. Is everything all right?"

I nod. "Panic attack." I reach into the seat back for the paper bag, open it, and put it in front of Rebecca's face. "Blow into this."

She swats it away. Then she says, miserably, between choked breaths, "What if it's too late?"

I stare at her. "What if it's too late to do what?"

Her eyes drift down, and meet mine. Her voice is a breath. "To get over you?"

My eyes fall over her cute nose, her long eyelashes, coated in tears, her watery eyes, and lips I'd kill to kiss again. "Why do you have to get over me?"

"But this can't…it isn't real. Eventually…eventually I'll have to. Right?"

"No," I say right away. Then louder: "No. Hell, no. We can keep this going. The great thing about this is, *we* write this story. I sure as hell don't want it to end, and it doesn't have to. Not even from fifteen hundred miles away."

Her chest heaves as she sucks in a breath. "You don't want it to?"

"Hell no. I told you I don't," I say, bringing my hand to her cheek. "I told you I'd knew if I had something special, and I wouldn't let it go. I want you to come to the premiere of my next movie. I really do."

She still looks doubtful. I brush my lips on hers, kissing her lightly.

"Will you come?"

She nods. "Yes."

I take her hand, squeezing it tight. "And you know the thing about *An Affair to Remember* and *Serendipity* and *Before Sunrise*?" I whisper to her. "They might have fucked everything up, sure. But you forgot something. They all end up where they belong in the end. Together."

The hard, stricken look in her eyes softens. "You're right. They do."

"So just relax, okay? Think about the premiere in April. We'll get all dressed up to the nines to watch shit get blown up. It'll be great."

A smile tugs at the corner of her lips.

She lays her head on my shoulder, and her breathing calms. In a few moments, her eyelashes begin to flutter, and while I've only known this woman slightly under two days, I know certain things. How she looks when she finally falls asleep, like an absolute angel. How even the touch of her hand sends sparks through my bloodstream. How I'm not going to take my eyes off her for one second during this three-hour flight.

And most of all, how I'm bound in something that isn't going to let me go in Dallas.

No fucking way.

chapter thirty-five

Becka

I wake just as the plane is landing, my head on Noah's shoulder, my hand in his.

He kisses the side of my head and says, "You were out like a light."

He lifts the window and I see the great state of Texas below us, speeding by in a blur as the plane descends lower and lower.

I look at him. He looks at me. In half an hour, we will walk out of these doors, into the terminal, find our connecting flights…and who knows if we will ever see each other again?

We will. Yes. It's happening.

Six months from now.

I think.

The plane lands without any drama. The only drama inside me is this overwhelming panic that the rest of my life, the only time I'll see him is as a two-dimensional figure on a movie screen. That I will never get to hold him, touch him, be with him in the flesh.

The plane taxis to the gate, and the fasten seatbelt light dings off. I reach for my phone and say, "I know you're busy. So don't call me. Don't text me. Just...delete my number, okay?"

He lifts his phone. "Why?"

"Because it'll be weird. Talking to you, with all that distance between us. I don't want to hear your voice and feel all frustrated that I can't see you, and I don't want us to fight because we're frustrated. Long distance never works. It just never does. So let's not."

"But we'll see each other again? At the premiere?"

I grab my bag, pull out the notebook. I rip a blank page out of it and write my address. I hand it to him. "If you still want me to come, send the ticket here."

"If?" He shakes his head. He takes the pen from me, and rips a corner off the page. "This is *my* address. If you want me to read your book when you finish it, send it to me."

I look at the address. Hollywood Hills. It sounds far too glamourous for me. But I'm keeping the faith here. It's better to hope and wish for six months and be let down in the end than to lose everything right now.

I pocket the address in my bag. "All right."

I can just see us, five months from now. Me, sitting there with a copy of my book, afraid to send it because Mr. High and Mighty will probably go, *Rebecca Who?* Him, hanging out in his hot tub in the Hollywood Hills, handing his premiere tickets to his latest flavor of the week, who happens to have a much cuter ass than mine.

I squelch the panic inside me as we rise to our feet.

It will be okay. Because even if it goes away, we had this. This one, perfect moment in time, where we were officially, one-hundred-percent, out-of-our-minds crazy about each other.

We are the last people off the plane. We take our time, leisurely checking over and over again to make sure we didn't leave anything behind.

When we start to walk down the aisle, he lets me go first, his hand solidly on the small of my back, like I belong to him. I've never felt so protected. So wanted. So loved.

We say goodbye to the flight attendants, the pilots.

We step off the plane.

He falls in step next to me as we walk up the gangway, to the terminal.

"Where is your connecting flight?" he asks as we find ourselves landed in Terminal A.

I check my ticket. "This terminal. I have a couple hours. What about yours?"

"Terminal B. Leaving in…forty minutes."

"Oh. I guess you've got to…"

His hand is around mine, not anywhere near letting go. "Let me see you safely to your gate, first."

I smile at him. My gate's right there, in the distance, in the opposite direction of the Skylink, which he needs to take to the other terminal. But I let him. I'll do anything to squeeze out just another few minutes.

We walk as slowly as possible. Dragging our feet like two old people. Commuters swerve around us, anxious to get wherever they need to go, but we ignore them.

When we get there, he looks at his phone. He says, "I guess this really is it."

I nod.

"Okay. No phone calls. Just...premiere tickets. Coming your way in April."

"Yes. And I'll send you my book, as soon as I finish."

"Good."

He looks at me like a package he can't wait to unwrap. He sucks in a breath, and I breathe in in anticipation of this last kiss. I know I will want to take a snapshot of it so I can try to do it justice in my books. I know it will be over too quickly. I know I will want more the second it ends.

His hand tangles in my hair, pulling me to him. And then he's kissing me, and everything around us dissolves. Kissing me so hard that it takes my breath but fills me with something better. His hands are in my hair and down my back and everywhere and it just doesn't feel like enough.

When I taste the salt I realize I'm crying. I pull away from him and I swipe at my eyes.

"Hey," he says. "Hey."

And I can't see, the tears are blurring everything so much. My throat is choked so I nod to let him know I'm okay. Or... will be okay.

I'm just not right now.

He takes my face in both hands. Presses his forehead against mine. "Listen to me." And then he does it. He affects Brock's voice and says, 'Even if you don't got your bases full, going home is still damn sweet.' Right?"

Oh, god, I'm going to ugly cry soon. I nod and close my eyes. Then whisper, "Just go. Don't miss your flight again," turning away, before I become a snotty mess.

He turns. He starts to leave.

I know I'm unleashing Niagara Falls, but I can't help it. I look back at him, and he's walking backwards, watching me, waving, in a dare of who will turn around first.

Neither of us does. Little by little, people begin swerving between us, until he's swallowed up by the crowd. I crane my head to see him, but I only catch a flash of sandy hair, a glimpse of his jacket—never him in whole—before he disappears.

I find a chair at my gate and sink down into it, watching as my plane arrives at the gate. The plane that will take me in what feels like the wrong direction.

I pull out my phone, glancing at it, for the time. I still have an hour before boarding. I open up my Facebook, but it doesn't hold my interest. I reach for my laptop, but I don't think I can concentrate right now. Not when every minute that passes means Noah is getting farther and farther from me.

Did I really think I could write this book, without him? Without my muse?

Everything around me is so very dull. And…constricting. The walls are angling in, threatening to fall upon me and crush me to death.

I'm starting to remember why I hated airports.

chapter thirty-six

Noah

I walk backwards, waving to her, until I stumble on someone's foot. I pause for an apology and the second I look up again, she's gone, lost in a crowd of people.

I turn away. Six months. Less than that. She can finish up that book, and I can get my career under control. This'll be good.

I walk down the concourse, toward the Skylink, my head never far away from the feeling of her skin against mine. My cock, buried inside her. The sweet, soft noises she'd made as she came. The uniquely cute-sexy way she did just about everything, from walking to brushing her teeth to…fuck. Everything.

Real. True. There isn't a woman on earth that could move me like that.

I go into Hudson News, thinking I need something—a hell of a lot of something—to take her off my mind. The only thing that even strikes my fancy—the thing that I pick up and actually consider buying, even though I read it in eighth grade and it's beyond agonizing—is fucking *Silas Marner*.

What the hell is wrong with me?

I need to concentrate on my auditions. That's my main objective, now. There's no doubt something in me has shifted. Something I think I can definitely use to deliver the goods with my next audition.

But my skin is crawling, itching with a need that I can't define. A desire to move, to seek something out. Someone.

I reach the entrance to the Skylink and start to pace, since I can't stand still. My muscles are tight, my stomach clenched.

I force myself to plant my feet and see a couple who must be on vacation, standing hand in hand. She stands on her tiptoes and kisses him, gazing deep into his eyes.

And all I can think is, *I had that once.*

Once.

And as usual, Rebecca's fucking right.

Once in a lifetime doesn't happen twice.

chapter thirty-seven

Becka

It only takes about five minutes.

It starts the second he disappears from view. I heave a sigh and try to wipe the tears away and tell myself that it's okay. That I'll see him again. That absence will make the heart grow fonder. All those good things.

I remind myself that I have a book to write, and now I have the tools and the motivation to write it. I tell myself I'll be so busy that those six months will go by like lightning.

I think about how amazing the premiere will be. I'll get myself this dress that will level Megalith's stone jaw to the ground. Hobnob with people like JLaw. Walk the plush red carpet and have everyone wonder if I'm *someone*. Meet Noah again for the first time in one hundred and sixty-three days and have the most incredible reunion sex that even Aphrodite will weep.

Then I start thinking about those six months. One hundred and sixty-three nights. Without him.

I do the math on my calculator. He's been gone five minutes. I only have forty-six thousand, nine hundred and forty-four of those left.

Holy god.

At that thought, my throat starts to constrict. My pulse pounds in my temple and my head aches. I reach for the water bottle he'd bought for me, clutching it, twisting the lid.

I try to force a sip down my throat, but my vision starts to swim.

Oh, no.

Five minutes. And I already know I've made the wrong decision by leaving him. I already know that fifty years from now, when I look back to see what I did wrong, I will see this as the moment that my life veered off-track. What was that shit about not texting or calling? At least it would be *something*.

I had something amazing. And I just threw it away, tossed it up into the air and said, "Come back later." Who does that?

My breathing comes fast and shallow. I lean over, burying my head between my knees. The edges of my vision go dark.

"Are you okay, miss?" someone asks me in a thick southern twang.

"I'm... I don't..."

People are moving around me, but I can't focus on them. My eyes are on my feet, but there are fireworks exploding in my vision. I hear voices, raised in confusion.

"Everyone. Stand back. We've called a paramedic. It looks like she might faint."

chapter thirty-eight

Noah

Fuck this.

chapter thirty-nine

Becka

Someone hands me a paper bag. I'm just bringing it to my lips when I hear a familiar voice.

"It's okay. She's with me."

I swing my head up so fast that I hit him square in the jaw. He reels back, wraps his arm around me, and pulls me against his body. "Hey. You okay?"

"Noah?" I sob, hardly believing this is true. "What are you doing here? Did you miss your flight?"

"No." His hands are on me, steadying me. "Well, yeah, but I meant to do it, this time."

"You did?"

"Yeah. Fuck the Some Day. Let's do the Right Now."

I stare at him. "Are you…"

"Don't say we can't. I may have neglected to tell you a little about Hollywood. Sure, it's pretty much the most batshit place you'll ever see. But the thing is, creative types live there because it's really inspiring. I mean, take my house. It's huge.

It has a lot of feng shui in it to stimulate the senses, get the blood flowing. Trust me on this. I get the feeling that if you start writing there, you'll never stop."

I look up at him from the tears in my eyes. "Really?"

"Totally. So that's why I think you need to come with me. For a few days. Or a week. Or until you finish the book. Or forever. Whatever you want. When it comes to inspiration, fuck Manhattan. Hollywood is where it's at."

He's babbling so adorably, breathlessly, that it suddenly all makes sense. Suddenly I can't imagine that there was ever any other option. "Yes."

"And I'll give you your own office, if you want. So you can be alone. Or with me. Or whatever. Just say you'll—" He stops. "Wait. You said yes?"

I nod. My answer was yes the second he walked away from me, when I knew I was making the biggest mistake of my life. "But…why? Why did you come back?"

"Because." He smiles and touches my face. And it's Brock's words, but it's his voice, this time, all Noah. "You don't give up when the thing you love hangs in the balance. You dig deeper. You taught me that, Rebecca."

"You…love me?" I ask him.

He lifts me up and kisses me. "Turns out, I can't board a flight without you on it. So I'd say…fuck, yes." He grins at me, brings a finger to my lips, stroking my chin so gently, eyes flitting over my features like he can't believe I'm real. "And guess what?"

My voice comes out breathlessly, in three syllables. "Wh-a-t?"

"That was our black moment. I think we're in the clear."

I let out a gasp that's partly a laugh. He's right. And I think it would make a great scene in a book.

Because everyone gathered around us, previously worried about my medical condition, lets out a collective sigh. And as he lowers his lips onto mine, slowly this time, and I have no intention of letting him go…they all burst into a round of applause.

"Take your bow," I murmur into his skin.

But he doesn't. He just keeps me in his arms, his mouth on me in this crazy sexy kiss that doesn't appear to have an end.

We'll have to change our tickets. *Again.* We'll probably be banned from ever taking another American flight again. Lily will have to keep watching Tibby and holding my mail and…whatever.

But I have the words in me. Now I know… I have the courage, the passion, and the inspiration, right here. Now, I can just let them out.

chapter forty

Noah

The new flight leaves at 7:20 p.m. It gets in at 9:40 p.m. Plenty of time to make it home for my six a.m. limo.

This is one flight I definitely plan to be on.

With Rebecca's head on my shoulder, I feel like I can take on the world. Megalith. Hamlet. Whatever else might come my way.

I place a kiss on her hairline. She's lazily paging through the fashion magazine, but every once in a while she looks up to smile at me. "Hey," I say to her.

"Hey, back."

I respond to Anne's latest message, where she arranged the publicity photos yet again, with: ***On my way. In Dallas now. Flight should be in by 10.***

She responds a moment later with: ***Hallelujah! Text me when you get in. You're wanted for an audition with a nice***

little indie project that's just come across my desk. I think you'll be pleased. Have a good flight.

It will be a good one. A damn good one. For one, Rebecca and I were able to get seats together.

So I'll be sitting in the best seat on the plane.

And I can't fucking wait. I can't wait to show her around Hollywood. To take her home to my bed. To see her cute little author ass, sitting in my house, typing away at her hot pink laptop.

I'll still hate being made into the big blue asshole. But it's not such a bad thing.

In fact, life is pretty damn sweet.

I lean down and kiss her again, because I can't get enough of her mouth. Her perfect, sweet mouth. And all the rest of her.

I've heard that you can't find heaven in hell.

Bullshit. Rebecca's living proof of that. My heaven. And I plan to keep it as close to me as possible, for as long as I can.

chapter forty-one

Becka

It's pretty late by the time the Uber drops us off in front of Noah's home in Hollywood Hills. Sprawling, modern, gorgeous, the one-story Architectural-Worthy mansion is dark as Noah takes my hand and leads me to the front doors.

"Ready?"

I nod, biting my lips from the nerves and excitement.

I'm going to live here. With Noah Steele.

I texted Lily on my way here.

Me: ***Lily, change of plans. I'm…moving in.***

Lily: ***Becka…are you drunk?***

Me: ***No, BUT I'M HIGH!!!!! ON HIM! ON THIS! ON LIFE!!***

My phone kept buzzing from then on, and I promised Lily I'd call her, and my renter, tomorrow. I know I have to tell my parents everything. Bryn. Everyone.

But right now, neither Noah is concerned about the rest of the world, nor am I.

We can't stop grinning, we can't stop reaching out and touching each other. We can't stop the feeling that we are exactly where we want to be—and with who we want to be.

As Noah now opens the thick mahogany doors with a click, he motions me inside.

"After you."

I step inside to be greeted by the most gorgeous view of the city of Los Angeles from the living room window. I hear Noah flip on the light-switch, and I'm greeted by a beautifully decorated modern bachelor home.

There's a granite bar at the end, elegant leather couches with dark cowhide pillows, and a black woven leather rug over elegant wood floors.

"It's beautiful." I can't stop drinking in every bit of his place. Because it's his. I can see pictures of his from his childhood. Magazines that he reads—*Hollywood Reporter*, *National Geographic*, and *Time*.

There are billboards of old movies on the wall, framed in sleek, modern black frames that match the décor.

"We can remove this guy." He motions to the posters.

"Are you kidding me? I love him!" I cry, shaking my head in warning. "I'll kill you if you remove him from our walls."

"Because you love him. You just said so. Literally."

He raises his brows, and I bite my lips and admit, "I love him. The actor. Not just the role."

Noah's ashy-gray eyes suddenly turn an intense steely-gray. He pulls me to him and drops a kiss on my lips, stealing his tongue inside. "How'd I get so lucky, Rebecca? Huh?" He looks down on me, both of us breathless from our kiss.

"When you figure it out, let me know. I'm trying to figure out the same thing."

We're both grinning like dopes until Noah seems to remember he still has the rest of the house to show me. He shows me the chef's kitchen—three times the one I have back in Austin—and the dining room, cinema room, and butler's quarters.

"No, I don't have a butler. But if we ever need some help after throwing a big party or whatever." He shrugs, as if it doesn't matter. Next he leads me back to the living room, and to a large shelf-lined room with a wall of windows and the same stunning city view.

"This is your office. It's mine, but I have no use for it. It's got a view." Noah opens the window to the terrace and the infinity pool that are also easily accessed from the living room.

We step out for a few minutes.

The breeze runs through my hair, and I'm drinking it all in with a daze that makes me keep wondering, *Is this really my life? Is this really happening to me?*

I hold my breath as the view of Hollywood spans out before me. My throat works as I struggle to say something, but no words come out.

Noah is behind me, his hands on my shoulders, his voice in my ear. "Are you scared?"

I finally get some words out. "More scared to let go of the best thing that's ever happened in my life."

"Come here." He grabs my hand in his and leads me back inside, past the living room, down a spacious hallway, to the double doors at the end. He rolls one open, leading me inside, to the massive king bed with a leather headboard. "And this…this is our bed."

He guides me down on the bed.

It's beautiful. Soft and plush, like heaven waiting for me.

"I don't want you wondering who's ever been in here with me. Because no one has. This is my space, and that's how I've always kept it. Keeps me sane."

I believe him, nod. Run my hands over his chest, under his t-shirt.

There's a long silence as I touch his skin, all while Noah looks down at me intently on his bed.

"Can't get enough of you, Rebecca."

"Me of you."

"God, I can't believe you're here with me." He nuzzles my stomach.

I giggle, and he laughs softly and eases back. He pulls off his t-shirt. Shakes off his jeans.

Oh yes, please.

All of Noah Steele for me.

Hard for me.

I drink him up like a starved girl. Sitting up in bed to frantically strip the most that I can. When he crawls over me, I'm still in my underwear and sort of caught with the straps of my bra. "Allow me." He smirks as he reaches out and unhooks my bra so I can slide it off more easily.

"Thank you." I hesitate, desperate to touch, not knowing where to start. I ease up and grab his jaw, setting a kiss on his lips. "Noah."

He takes my hand and turns it around, and sets a kiss on my palm. I curl my fingers around it as if to keep it there, always. "You're perfect here. I don't know what exact second I fell for you or when I knew, but I'll never let go of you."

"Me either."

"Now I want to eat you, Rebecca. Feast on you, Texas. Right here on our bed."

Oh god.

Our bed.

OUR. BED.

Because this is what we're doing. We're going to live together. Because he wants me, and I WANT him. He LOVES me. And I LOVE him.

I'm quivering as he reaches out to hook his thumb on the string of my underwear, tugging it down my legs.

"Now I know you're a writer and there are rules to a good romance—and the fact that you were willing to come with me… I don't want you thinking you're the only one making an effort here. So I want to give you an explosive welcome home. So you know how much I appreciate you feeling as strongly about us as I do. I promise I'll do everything possible not to make your prick list, ever. Give you what you deserve. Love you like you deserve."

I'm nodding fast, quivering as he parts my thighs. Noah keeps eye contact the whole time he lowers his head—and sets his lips on my sex lips.

I jerk from the contact.

Velvety. Wet. Warm. *Perfect.*

"Yes, god, Noah." I grab a fistful of sheets. They feel satiny, and so good…but not as good as his tongue as he licks it up and down my folds…then between them. A groan leaves me, my fingers tightening on the sheets as he slides one hand up the inside of my thigh, bringing his thumb into the fun. Letting his thumb twirl my clit as he licks into me…and then switching…letting his thumb dip inside me as his tongue rubs my clit in slow, languorous, excruciatingly delicious circles.

I'm dying and it's the best feeling ever. Oral was something I'd never really craved until him. I thought I'd feel vulnerable, and just…too helpless. I do feel vulnerable and helpless, but I feel loved and cherished with every stroke too.

There's no fucking way I'll stop him.

Even as I'm thinking that, in a daze, my hips are starting to thrust upward. To his glorious, wicked mouth. He's closing his eyes, as if he's too undone by my taste to keep eye contact any longer. My eyes drift shut, sensations overpowering me as I'm suddenly seized by my orgasm.

I gasp, coming hard and fast for him, the waves crashing through me.

Noah keeps on licking even as I thrash beneath him, slowing his strokes as I come back down. "You taste good, Texas." He lifts his head, his mouth glistening from my juices.

"Like what…" I pant out.

Noah drags his eyes along my breasts, along my face, as he curls my legs around his hips and then leans down to drop a path of kisses up my bare torso, up my neck, to my lips.

"Like coming home after a long, exhausting trip where everything went wrong except one thing," he murmurs, crushing my mouth beneath his as he drives home inside me. "You."

chapter forty-two

Becka

Six Months Later

I'd like to say that my time of endless waiting in an airport came to an end, after that.

But that isn't true.

Six months after I decided to follow Noah to Hollywood, we're at LAX once again. The sun is setting, and we're getting close to the time when Route 5 will be wall-to-wall cars. This time, we're checking the arrivals boards. Once again, standing still, while the whole world scurries around us.

"Was it delayed again?" Noah asks me as I come back to where he's sitting by a baggage claim carousel, reading a new script, this one for a Megalith spinoff movie. He has his legs out, crossed at the ankle, and is leisurely turning the pages, wearing his Clark Kent superhero glasses.

I have to sigh every time I look at him, he looks so damn good.

"I don't know," I reply. "I think it should have landed five minutes ago."

He removes his glasses and slips them into his pocket. We both look with great anticipation toward the terminal, where commuters are descending an escalator to claim their baggage.

No Lily.

Now, I'm pretty sure if I do see her, my first response will be to pinch her to make sure she's real.

We've been here for six, going on seven, hours. She was supposed to arrive in the morning, and I forgot to check to make sure her flight was on time. First, there were storms. Then, there was an issue with the plane. Three hours ago, Lily texted me that she was stuck on the tarmac and had been there an hour. ***I'm dying.***

I'd smiled to myself, then typed in: ***There are worse things than being stranded in an airport.***

To which she'd quickly responded: ***No hot actors here. MY seatmates are a harried mom and her toddler. YAY ME.***

I think of her and sigh. Poor Lily. She has been salivating for this trip, her first vacation since she started working as a law clerk at a firm where they pay her peanuts and expect her to work fourteen hours a day. I want everything to be perfect for her. She already loves Noah, since I brought him back with me a few months ago. But I want her to love this place as much as I do.

It's a damn good thing the premiere for *King of the Galaxy* isn't until tomorrow night. Lily's going to be tired. She'll need to freshen up, and I can show her all the sights that Noah showed me when I was new to town.

I kneel down in front of him as he sets his manuscript aside and picks up his phone. He studies it and says, "This says the plane is still in the air."

I groan.

He stretches, then pushes against the carousel and rises to his feet, the movement baring enough tanned, taut abdominal muscles that I sense all the women around him eyeing him with desire. It's something I've grown used to. But his gaze never leaves mine. "Want something to eat?"

I shake my head and pull my knees up to my chest, just as a little boy who can't be more than seven comes up to him. "Are you Noah Steele?" he asks timidly.

Noah nods and high fives him. "Hey, buddy." I smile at his mother who asks to take a picture. Noah does his Megalith fierce face and tells the boy to do the same. The result is frame-worthy, and makes my ovaries explode a little. I tell the mom to get in and snap a picture of the three of them.

"Thanks!" the kid says, all grins, and the mother grabs her son's hand as he skips away.

My phone buzzes with a text. I expect it to be Lily. But it's Bryn. ***Finished it in one day. OMG girl you are incredible!!***

I find myself grinning goofily. I know all my reviews won't be awesome like that, but it feels good to have this piece of work I made. To know that I brought these characters to life and people were invested in their story, even for just a little while.

Noah raises an eyebrow. "Lily?"

I shake my head. "Bryn. She just finished the book."

"And I take it she hated it as much as I did," he says with a sardonic grin. He's been my biggest champion since that first day, when he set me up in his office and called it mine, opened the glass doors, complete with a perfect view of the mountains and the city below, as well as a slushy drink with a little umbrella in it.

I sipped on it and drank in the scenery, inspired by love. And I did something brave again. As brave as following Noah to Hollywood. I discarded every bit I had of Ben and Leia, and realized it wasn't their story I needed to tell. It was ours. Noah's and mine. And I gave it to us, *we* gave it to us: our happily ever after and everything. I started the story as every story starts, with Chapter One, and one sentence.

New York can be a cruel, cruel city...

The rest was written 'in the stars' as Noah and I joke. In the end, we went for it. We took a plunge into the unknown, knowing only we wanted each other. And neither of us have had any regrets.

Bryn. I told her I moved in with Noah. I haven't been able to see her in person, but I promised her she'd know every little detail as soon as I wrote my book.

I didn't want to relate everything because the feelings were raw and alive, like a fire in the pit of my belly, and I wanted to unleash it, one word at a time. Now she knows about it all.

Revisions took some time, and searching for the perfect title, but now, *Muse* is ready for the whole world to see. I'm nervous, but mostly excited.

So, so excited.

About the book, my first movie premiere and everything else.

And everything in my life touches Noah. I've been home to Austin since that day, but I always come back to him. In fact, we haven't been apart more than a couple days.

I'm not sure how I'm going to cope when he leaves for London, next week, to start filming of the movie version of *We Will Rock You,* which is a musical containing songs from Queen. He gets to sing.

The boy's got pipes. Like, so good I can barely stand to watch him. Whenever he sings to me, it turns me into one of those Beatles groupies who faints or has to cover her face with a pillow to stop from dying from pure excitement.

Noah rakes his hands through his hair and paces a little ways away. Then he saunters back, lifting his arms and crossing them over his head. "I think I might go crazy here."

I stand up. "Airports are not such bad places," I tell him. "Remember?"

He grins. "How can I forget?"

I put my arms around his neck, then stand on my tiptoes to nibble on that delicious place where his jaw meets his earlobe. He smells like shaving cream and tastes slightly salty, and as I press up against him I feel my body responding, my nipples hardening under my tank top.

He slides his palms down my back to crush my body against his. His hands slip over my ass, and he squeezes. I wriggle. I don't mind PDAs quite so much now, but I know what this will lead to. It's unquenchable. And if we continue to go down this maddening path, the police and indecent exposure charges might be in our future. Megalith might have fans in high places, but he also has a ton of tabloids who'd just love to catch his stone ass *in flagrante*. Hell, they already once caught us going through the drive-in at Jack in the Box. Big story. *Yes, it's true, the man of stone eats fast food!*

He tightens his hands around me, and slips and hand under the hem of my tank, stroking his fingers along the bare skin at the small of my back. "There are places we can be alone here."

I look around and see a sign in the corner of the room, near the car rental desks. The family restroom.

Lily's probably still in the air. Besides, if not, she'll totally understand. This is Megalith, we're talking about, here. Man of stone. You should see what he did to the Golden Gate Bridge. What he wants, he usually gets.

I take his hand, leading the way, and we easily escape into the room, unnoticed.

He flips on the light. "This brings back memories."

Then he presses the door closed, and twists the lock.

I'm on him before he turns, kissing him so he falls back against the door, reaching for the hem of his t-shirt so that I can get my hands over those delicious muscles.

His hands delve below my skirt and come up over my thighs, kneading the muscles of my ass. His fingers blaze a trail of heat on my skin, wherever they touch.

He dips his head to lick at my mouth, and his hands come around, framing my face. His eyes take me in like I'm the most precious and beautiful thing he's ever seen. "You beautiful thing, you," he murmurs. "You take me places, Rebecca."

I kiss him, hold him tight, and relax into his sexy, wicked mouth, letting myself be devoured by him. I've been to the most surprising places in this country with him, and he's right…it's never been the place.

And he's the person.

THE END

DEAR READERS,

Thanks so much for reading *Muse*. If you enjoyed it, please consider leaving a review. It helps other readers discover my stories, and spreading the love gives good karma too! Hope you enjoyed Becka and Noah's story as much as I did writing it. I've always wanted to write a story that takes place in a short amount of time, where every second counts, and the clock is ticking before our couple needs to part! Hope you enjoyed it like I did!

Here's to you and your muse, whoever and whatever that is.

XOXO,

Katy

acknowledgments

Although writing is a personal thing and sometimes quite a lonely profession, publishing is a whole other beast, and I couldn't do it without the help and support of my amazing team. I'm grateful to you all.

To my family, I love you!

Thank you Amy and everyone at Jane Rotrosen Agency!

Thank you to my editors, copy editors, proofer, and betas: Kelli, CeCe, Anita, Mara, Monica, Nina, and Kim.

Thank you Nina, Jenn, Shannon, Hilary, Chanpreet, and everyone at Social Butterfly PR.

Thank you Melissa,

Gel,

my fabulous audio publisher,

and my fabulous foreign publishers.

Special thanks to Sara at Okay Creations for the beautiful cover.

Thank you Julie for formatting,

to all of my bloggers for sharing and supporting my work—I value you more than words can say!

And readers—I'm truly blessed to have such an enthusiastic, cool crowd of people to share my books with. Thank you for the support. xo.

Katy

about

New York Times, *USA Today*, and *Wall Street Journal* bestselling author Katy Evans is the author of the Manwhore, Real, and White House series. She lives with her husband, two kids, and their beloved dogs. To find out more about her and her books, visit her pages. She'd love to hear from you.

Website:
www.katyevans.net

Facebook:
https://www.facebook.com/AuthorKatyEvans

Twitter:
@authorkatyevans

Book Bub:
https://www.bookbub.com/authors/katy-evans

Sign up for Katy's newsletter:
http://www.katyevans.net/newsletter/

titles by katy evans

TYCOON MOGUL

MUSE

White House series:

MR. PRESIDENT COMMANDER IN CHIEF

WHITE HOUSE – BOXED SET

Manwhore series:

MANWHORE MANWHORE +1

MS. MANWHORE LADIES' MAN

WOMANIZER PLAYBOY

Real series:

REAL MINE

REMY ROGUE

RIPPED LEGEND

RACER